"Moving in with me makes perfect sense...."

Cooper continued, "Living together would be the easiest and fastest way to convince people we're a couple—and you did assure me that's what you want your boss to think."

"I want to convince him you're serious about me," Hannah replied. "I don't want him to get the idea that I've gone totally insane."

"There's nothing insane about it. Anyway, Hannah, I invited you to live with me, not sleep with me."

She was wary. "You're not trying to blackmail me into bed?"

Leigh Michaels has always loved happy endings. Even when she was a child, if a book's conclusion didn't please her, she'd make up one of her own. And though she always wanted to write fiction, she very sensibly planned to earn her living as a newspaper reporter. That career didn't work out, however, and she found she ended up writing for Harlequin Mills & Boon instead—in the kind of happy ending only a romance novelist could dream up!

Leigh likes to hear from her readers. You can write to her at P.O. Box 935, Ottumwa, Iowa, 52501-0935, U.S.A.

Books by Leigh Michaels

A CONVENIENT AFFAIR
Leigh Michaels

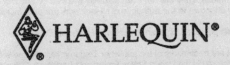

HARLEQUIN®

TORONTO • NEW YORK • LONDON
AMSTERDAM • PARIS • SYDNEY • HAMBURG
STOCKHOLM • ATHENS • TOKYO • MILAN • MADRID
PRAGUE • WARSAW • BUDAPEST • AUCKLAND

ISBN 0-373-03656-6

A CONVENIENT AFFAIR

First North American Publication 2001.

This edition published by arrangement with Harlequin Books S.A.

® and TM are trademarks of the publisher. Trademarks indicated with ® are registered in the United States Patent and Trademark Office, the Canadian Trade Marks Office and in other countries.

Visit us at www.eHarlequin.com

Printed in U.S.A.

CHAPTER ONE

UNTIL that morning, Hannah had started to think it didn't matter what hour of the day or night she walked Mrs. Patterson's dog. If she abruptly decided to take Brutus out at two o'clock in the morning, she'd no doubt still run headlong into Cooper Winston somewhere along the way.

When she stopped to think about it, however, Hannah concluded that the wee hours of the morning were actually one of the more likely times to encounter the occupant of the penthouse condominium. In the hours after midnight, he was apt to be just coming home to Barron's Court from a date... "And other associated activities," Hannah added under her breath.

Of course, she had also run into him at the crack of dawn, at high noon, and at nine-fifteen in the evening. The time seemed to be immaterial, the encounter inevitable.

Today, however, the chain appeared to have been broken. She and Brutus had gone all the way from Barron's Court up Grand Avenue to the governor's mansion and back, encountering their share of commuters and joggers and even a few bundled-up babies taking their mothers out for an airing in the autumn sunshine. But for once Hannah hadn't caught so much as a glimpse of a dark-haired, gray-eyed, broad-shouldered, supercilious six-foot hunk of testosterone named Cooper Winston.

By the time they once more reached the lobby of the condo complex, Brutus was breathing hard and Hannah could feel a glow throughout her whole body from the exercise and the crisp October breeze. She punched the button to summon the elevator and bent to release the pug's leash from his collar. "If you wouldn't pull so hard," she reminded him, "you wouldn't be so out of breath at the end of your walk."

She hadn't heard the Art Deco doors open, but even before the man inside the elevator stepped into the lobby, she knew he was there. *So much for thinking my luck has changed,* she thought, and slowly straightened up, turning to face Cooper Winston.

She wasn't sure precisely why the hair at the back of her neck always stood straight up the moment he appeared on the scene. Probably sheer dislike, Hannah thought, coupled with a touch of apprehension—for there was no doubt that lately she was the one who had been coming out the worse for wear in their encounters. Whatever the reason, it was certainly a negative one; it wasn't as if there was anything she found magnetically attractive about the man.

Not that he was exactly hard on the eyes, she admitted. The first time she'd encountered him—over a negotiating table at Stephens & Webster, where she was an associate attorney—Hannah had thought Cooper Winston was extremely good-looking. She was partial to tall men with black hair and curly eyelashes and chiseled features. But of course that had been before she'd encountered the tight-set jaw, the perpetual crease between his brows, and the icy silver of his gaze.

All of which were in evidence right now.

She considered asking him—sweetly, of course—if he'd drunk his vinegar for breakfast as usual. But since there was nothing to be gained by gratuitous insults, she looked through him instead and said with cool politeness, "Good morning, Mr. Winston."

He didn't answer. She felt his gaze slide over her, and she was suddenly and painfully aware of her tousled hair, her wind-reddened cheeks, her far-from-new sweatsuit, and the faint aroma of dog that she'd acquired when she'd scooped up Brutus and carried him across Grand Avenue to beat a stream of traffic.

If the man dared to make a comment…

She looked straight at him, her chin held high.

Cooper didn't say a word. He didn't have to, Hannah thought bitterly. One dark eyebrow, lifting just a fraction of an inch, said it all.

At her feet, Brutus growled.

Cooper looked down. "You no doubt have some logical reason why this animal isn't on a leash, Ms. Lowe."

"Brutus has never bitten you," she pointed out.

"He's threatened often enough."

"Only because you make it so plain that you don't like him."

"What's to like? He's ugly, overweight, and ill-tempered."

"Being ugly isn't his fault," Hannah said crisply. "All pugs are. And if you were locked up all day, every day, in Mrs. Patterson's teeny little apartment, you'd probably be—" She bit her tongue, but it was already too late.

Cooper's voice was silky. "Overweight, too? And even more ill-tempered than I already am?"

"I didn't say that."

"What a nice compliment you've paid Mrs. Patterson. She's quite a powerful woman, if merely being in her company could have such a destructive effect."

"Wait a minute! If you think I was saying that Mrs. Patterson is—" Hannah sputtered to a stop. He'd done it again, she admitted, irritated. Without even trying, he'd put her squarely in the wrong—and it wasn't much comfort to know that this time she'd handed him the opportunity.

"I'm sure you wouldn't dream of saying anything

against Mrs. Patterson, Ms. Lowe. At least not where she might hear about it."

Hannah bristled. "I simply meant that her arthritis keeps her from taking Brutus for walks, so of course he's fat and irritable and not well-conditioned."

"But you've been exercising him for weeks now," Cooper pointed out, "and though he does seem to have slimmed down and stopped wheezing like a hippo, he's still in a bad mood all the time. What does that say about your company, Ms. Lowe?"

She smiled up at him. "Are you ever going to forgive me for interfering with your agreement to sell that restaurant chain, Mr. Winston? After all, I was only looking after my client's best interests. And the sale did eventually go through as you'd arranged, even though the terms were slightly altered."

"That's what you call *slightly altered?* Ms. Lowe, I'll forgive you about the same time I forget the fifteen million bucks your interference cost me."

Hannah feigned a sigh of relief. "Then, since fifteen million is pocket change to a man like you, I must be well on the way to rehabilitation."

"Fifteen million," he mused, "and all because you batted your eyelashes like an ingenue and asked a last-minute, breathless, innocent-sounding question."

"It wasn't like that."

"You mean it wasn't as innocent as it sounded? I'm glad you're at least admitting to being cold and calculating." He didn't give her an opportunity to answer, but strode across the lobby toward the street.

Just as well, Hannah thought. Brutus had only growled at him, as usual; Hannah herself would have been tempted to bite the man if he'd kept it up.

On the fifth floor, she delivered Brutus to his owner and

with regret refused a cup of coffee. Then, rather than wait for the elevator again and risk the chance that instead of leaving for the day Cooper had only been going to the convenience shop down the street for a newspaper, Hannah took the fire stairs up two flights and walked down the hall to Isobel's condo.

Isobel's condo. Even though Hannah had lived there for nearly three months now, she still didn't call it home.

She paused just inside the door, bracing herself to face the silence. The rooms had never been quiet like this when Isobel was alive. But it had been almost exactly a month since Isobel had gone to a friend's house in Windsor Heights one afternoon to play bridge—and never came back.

It seemed to Hannah that the condo which had been Isobel's home for so many years was waiting for her to return. The sofa cushions were still crushed as if she had stood up just moments ago. The magazine she'd been reading lay facedown on the fainting couch in her silk-draped bedroom. The satin and lace peignoir she'd taken off when she'd dressed for her bridge party that last afternoon still lay across the foot of her bed. Bath powder still dusted the glass top of her mirrored dressing table.

Even the musky scent of Isobel's perfume had hardly faded; it seemed to be embedded in everything she'd owned, and every time Hannah opened a drawer or a closet she released a new cloud of fragrance.

It might have been a little easier to make the transition, Hannah thought, if she herself had lived there for more than a couple of months before Isobel died. But she'd still felt pretty much like a guest on the day Isobel's heart had abruptly given out—cautious of every action and every word, trying her best not to get in her elderly hostess's way or upset Isobel's longstanding routines. Now, living alone in Isobel's condo, Hannah felt like an intruder.

She'd intended to move out immediately, but that was more easily said than done, considering the shortage of apartments in the city just now and the prices they commanded.

Besides, when she'd mentioned the move to her boss at the law firm, Brenton Bannister had simply shaken his head. "It isn't as if you don't have a right to be there till the estate is settled," he'd said. "Your aunt was one of our clients, and I'm sure Ken Stephens would prefer to have the condo occupied—especially by someone he can trust—than to leave all of Isobel's treasures there unprotected while he deals with the paperwork and gets everything in order."

"She wasn't my aunt, she was a distant cousin," Hannah had reminded him. "And Barron's Court is the most exclusive condo complex in the city. It's not exactly a high-crime district."

But Brenton had only smiled at her as if she'd said something terribly witty, and the next day he assured her that he'd spoken to the senior partner who had been Isobel's attorney and gotten approval for Hannah to stay on.

So Hannah had stayed, but her discomfort hadn't lessened as the weeks went by. Every time she touched one of Isobel's possessions—even if she was only moving it out of her way—she had to fight off a superstitious shiver. And it might take months to sort out Isobel's estate; there appeared to be no end to the things the woman had owned.

Regardless of what Brenton thought about her rights, Hannah decided, it was past time to find another place to live.

Of course, she'd never find anything as nice or as con-

venient to the office as Barron's Court was, even if she
could afford the price such a place would cost. But even
if she ended up living in a cracker box, at least she
wouldn't be running into Cooper Winston all the time.
That would be the biggest benefit of all.

Wherever Cooper had gone that morning, it wasn't far
enough for Hannah's taste—because when she pushed
open the lobby door, her nemesis was standing under the
portico, obviously waiting for his car to be brought around
from the garage at the back of the complex.

She almost drew back in order to avoid him, knowing
that the parking valets wouldn't keep him waiting long.
But Brenton would be along any minute to pick her up for
the short ride to work, and he wasn't known for patience
any more than Cooper was. So Hannah gritted her teeth
and went out into the crisp autumn air.

The portico wasn't very large, so Hannah found herself
standing uncomfortably close to Cooper.

His gaze slid slowly over her emerald green suit, the
best-quality item her wardrobe boasted. "I must say I like
that fashion ensemble better than the one which includes
the dog. I realize it isn't saying much, but—"

"You know," Hannah mused, "your grandfather would
have done us all a favor, when he remodeled this building
into condos, if he'd provided separate front entrances."

A sleek red sports car pulled up in the fire lane and
Brenton Bannister lowered the passenger-side window and
leaned across the seat. "Good morning, Winston. Can I
offer you a lift?"

Hannah wondered for an instant if he seriously expected
Cooper Winston to fold himself into the sports car's tiny
rear seat, or if Brenton had forgotten about her altogether.

"They're bringing my car around now," Cooper said. "But thank you."

"You don't carry any hard feelings over that last little deal, I hope," Brenton probed.

"Not where *you're* concerned." Cooper opened the passenger door of Brenton's car with a flourish and held out a hand as if to help Hannah get in.

Or to push me into the street, Hannah thought. She avoided his touch, though she thanked him with elaborate politeness.

As the car pulled away from the curb, Brenton said, "He's mellowing. I thought he would, given a little time. He's a businessman, and he knows you can't always win on every point."

Hannah stared at him in disbelief. Hadn't he heard the irony in Cooper's voice? "*Mellowing?* I suppose you think Mount Rushmore is made of blue cheese, too."

"Hannah, you'll never get Winston's business with that attitude."

"Stephens & Webster will never get his business at all."

"Why not?"

"After all the money we cost him last time around—"

"Fifteen million is peanuts to Cooper Winston," Brenton said comfortably. "Anyway, that's precisely my point. As soon as he cools off, he'll want us on his team because we're demonstrably better than the firm he was using. *They* never anticipated that little loophole."

Hannah bit her tongue. It wasn't her job to try to break through Brenton's delusions.

"And just think, Hannah—that deal was a very small one, relatively speaking. There will be more. When Winston's monolith swallowed up its rival in that merger deal, they got all kinds of side businesses that they won't want to keep. The restaurant chain our client bought was only a fraction of the package. There's a shipping firm and the aircraft refitters and a string of nursing homes—'' He was practically drooling at the thought.

''I think it's a little early to start looking for buyers,'' Hannah said dryly. ''He said good morning, he didn't offer us a retainer.''

''It still wouldn't hurt to be nice to him,'' Brenton argued.

Yes, it would, Hannah thought. It would hurt a great deal. Compared to the effort involved in being nice to Cooper Winston, suffering through an impacted wisdom tooth would be like winning a prize.

Within two hours of arriving at work, Hannah was beginning to feel as if she'd been buried alive in the law library archives. Her table, located in the farthest corner, was surrounded by boxes stuffed with crumbling documents, and each time she moved a page, the musty aroma made her want to sneeze.

The first few days of digging through Jacob Jones's old files hadn't been so bad, but with each passing hour her claustrophobia seemed to grow worse. This case was nowhere near as interesting as the transfer of the restaurant chain had been.

But so long as she was merely an associate, the lowest-level attorney the firm had, the tedious details would fall to her. The restaurant case had had its dull days, too, she reminded herself. In fact, it had been pretty much routine right up until the instant before the deal was consummated, when Hannah had thought of one more small thing to be considered. The one small thing which everyone else, on both sides, had overlooked completely. The one small thing which had cost Cooper Winston fifteen million dollars.

Brenton Bannister poked his head around the corner of a bookshelf. "How's it going?"

"Not very well. I haven't found a shred of evidence yet to support our client's case."

"Don't sweat it just now." He perched on the corner of her table.

Hannah looked at him in disbelief. What on earth did he have on his mind to make him suddenly regard the Jones case as insignificant?

"Ken Stephens wants to see you in his office this morning," Brenton said briskly. "It's about your Aunt Isobel's estate."

"Cousin," Hannah said automatically.

"What?"

"I've told you before, Isobel wasn't my aunt, she was my grandfather's cousin."

"Aunt, cousin, whatever." Brenton shrugged. "I suggest you hurry right upstairs and find out what he wants. You don't keep a senior partner waiting."

"Why take up his time at all? He sent a message through you to say I could stay in the condo. I wonder why he didn't just do the same to tell me it's time to leave."

"Don't be silly," Brenton scoffed. "You're too important for that kind of treatment now."

Hannah frowned. "Important? What do you mean?"

Brenton hesitated, as if he'd said more than he'd intended. Then he shrugged. "Just a guess. Considering how agreeable he was about you staying on in the first place, I'm betting Isobel left you the condo."

Hannah shook her head. "I doubt she'd will her home

to a distant cousin whom she'd met for the first time just weeks before she died.''

"Why not?" Brenton said coolly. "Who else is there to inherit it? Anyway, she invited you to move in with her—which is more togetherness than a lot of elderly people would offer their young relatives. She must have had something of the sort in mind."

"I think," Hannah mused, "that she saw a chance to acquire a personal maid and social secretary for the cost of room and board. Not that I minded helping out, but there never was a time she didn't have a list of things for me to do. Letters to write and phone calls to return and errands to run and even canapés to hand around when she entertained—''

Brenton laughed. "Maybe this is her way of paying you back. From everything I've heard about Isobel, waiting to reward you till she was certain she wouldn't need the money anymore would be right down her alley."

Hannah had to smile, for Brenton was unquestionably right. Her elderly relative had been anything but the fluffy, generous, grandmotherly type.

"Anyway, Ken Stephens is waiting for you." Brenton slid off the corner of the table and added casually, "I'll be tied up with clients all afternoon. But I'll take you out to dinner tonight at the Flamingo Room and you can tell me all about it."

Hannah was startled. In the months she'd worked under Brenton's supervision, they'd spent countless evenings together over pizza or Chinese takeout and one case or another, and they'd grown to be friends. He'd taken her to the theater for her birthday, and she'd taken him to a concert for his. But there was something different about this invitation. Perhaps it was the restaurant he'd chosen—the nicest one in the city. Or perhaps it was something in the tone of his voice…

Her surprise must have registered in her face, for Brenton suddenly looked as self-conscious as a schoolboy. "We'll make a special evening of it. A very special evening. Over the last few months, Hannah, as I've gotten to know you…" He cleared his throat. "But you haven't got time for that now. You can't keep Ken Stephens waiting."

Hannah brushed the musty scent of Jacob Jones's files off her suit as best she could and took the elevator to the uppermost level of Stephens & Webster's three floors, to the most-prized corner office belonging to the senior partner.

She was still a bit dazed by Brenton's declaration of love—if, indeed, that was what it was. But what else could he have meant?

As I've gotten to know you… A very special evening…

The very idea that Brenton might actually be serious about her created an all-gone sensation in the pit of Hannah's stomach. She wasn't sure she liked it. She'd looked on him as a friend, that was all. If he wanted their relationship to be more—

But she'd deal with that later, she told herself. Right now, she needed to concentrate on Ken Stephens and whatever he had to say about Isobel's estate.

And who knew? Maybe Brenton was right after all and Isobel had left her something. Not the condo at Barron's Court, of course—that was far too much to expect. But it wouldn't take much of an inheritance right now to make a big difference in Hannah's life.

Ken Stephens's waiting room was a great deal larger than the cubicle Hannah used as an office, and it was far more luxurious. Furthermore, the young woman who sat at his secretary's desk was much better dressed than Hannah herself was.

But then—unlike Hannah—Ken Stephens's daughter didn't have law school loans to repay, so she could afford designer clothes. Of course, that begged the question of what Kitty Stephens was doing here at all; if she was in the habit of acting as her father's secretary, Hannah had never heard about it.

Hannah took a chair and entertained herself by making a mental list of the things she would buy, if indeed Isobel had left her a small legacy. A few more really good suits would be first. Clothes might make the man, as the old saying went, but they could destroy a woman. A man could get by with a minimally stocked closet and a good dry cleaner, since one masculine pinstriped suit looked so very much like another. A professional woman, on the other hand, needed a wide variety if she wasn't to get looks of the sort Cooper Winston had given her this morning.

Not that her desire for new clothes had anything to do with him. For all she cared, he could look at her in the same green suit from now till Armageddon. After all, he didn't have to pay attention to what she wore.

And it wasn't that she was getting her hopes up for a legacy, either. She was just killing time. So much for Brenton's idea that Ken Stephens was waiting for her; it was too bad she hadn't thought to bring along a carton of Jacob Jones's old receipts so she could keep working. But of course the musty smell would hardly have been a welcome addition to the senior partner's waiting room.

A chime on the secretary's desk sounded, and—looking bored—Kitty Stephens waved a hand toward the heavy door of the inner office.

Hannah tapped and went in.

Behind a desk that was roughly the size of Hannah's

entire cubicle, a silver-haired man half rose and pointed toward a pair of chairs pulled up directly across the polished surface from him. "Have a seat, Ms. Lowe. I'm sorry to have interrupted your day. I understand you're working with Bannister on the Jones case now."

Hannah smiled faintly. "I wouldn't say I'm *working with,* exactly. I'm simply going through all the papers so I can brief him on the background before the case comes to trial."

"Well, that's the kind of support we rely on our young associates to provide." His gaze coolly assessed Hannah. "I understand you're also the genius who caused a bit of a panic at the last minute over Cooper Winston's restaurant chain."

Hannah wished that he'd made it sound more like a compliment. "Yes, sir."

"Our client was quite grateful. I thought you'd like to know." He leaned back in his chair. "In a few minutes we'll get started on tidying up the details concerning Isobel's estate. But in the meantime, tell me how you came to be living with her. I'm afraid I never knew the fine points."

And as Isobel's attorney, he probably would have known all about me, Hannah thought, *if Isobel had left me anything of significance.* Obviously, it was a good thing she'd never really gotten her hopes up—much less decided what color her new suits should be.

"It's quite simple," Hannah said. "When I first came to town, of course, I was very busy with my new job here at the firm. But after a few months, I went to visit Isobel. It was just a social thing, really, to go and pay my respects to a senior member of the family."

"You'd known her for some time, then? Years, perhaps?"

"Actually, no. I mean, I knew her name, of course, but I'd never met her before. It hasn't been a very close family. And it wasn't a very close relationship, either—she was my grandfather's cousin—but since much of my family is gone, I wanted to make contact with Isobel."

"So you visited her often?"

"No. Just the one time."

Ken Stephens sounded politely incredulous. "And on the strength of that one visit, she invited you to move in with her?"

Hannah's jaw tightened, and she had to make an effort to keep her voice level. "Yes, she did. It surprised me, too, at the time. I'd happened to mention that my room-mate was getting married and I was having trouble finding an apartment I both liked and could afford, and Isobel offered me a place to live for a while. I thought she meant that we could do each other a good turn. I could look after her a bit—"

"Look after Isobel?" Ken Stephens sounded astonished.

"Yes. Of course, that was before I knew her very well," Hannah pointed out. "It didn't take long to realize that the last thing Isobel wanted was to be treated as if she was elderly."

"Quite a nice little arrangement you had," he mused.

Hannah gritted her teeth. She was grateful that another tap on the door prevented her from saying something she was bound to regret.

"Now that you're both here," Ken Stephens said with satisfaction, "we can get started."

Hannah didn't even look around at the newcomer. She was still listening to Ken Stephens's last comment echoing in her mind. *A nice little arrangement you had,* he'd said. Past tense.

Well, it was no more than she'd expected. She'd sit

quietly though the formalities and start studying the classifieds over lunch...

The new arrival said, "Sorry I'm late, Stephens."

Hannah froze. *It's your imagination,* she told herself frantically. *There is no reason on earth for Cooper Winston to be here. This is Isobel's estate we're talking about, not some merger.*

But there was no denying, when she turned her head to look, that Cooper was standing just inside the office, one hand still on the door. Hannah noted that Kitty Stephens had not only stood up to show him to the door, but she'd ushered him all the way in. And he was looking down at her as if fascinated by the designer scarf at her throat—or, perhaps, the face it framed.

"Thank you," he said gently.

This was a different Cooper, Hannah thought. For one thing, it was the first time she'd seen him without the frown she had thought was permanently etched between his brows.

So was that irritable expression one he directed only at Hannah herself? Or was Kitty Stephens the exception, the one person who didn't inspire him to sarcasm?

"Thanks for coming, Winston," Ken Stephens said. "Kitty, see that we're not disturbed."

The secretary murmured, "Yes, Daddy," and withdrew.

Her shock diminishing, Hannah leaned back in her chair. "I didn't know you'd be here, Mr. Winston," she said, with her best sunny smile, "or I'd have brought your friend Brutus. Which brings me to the question of why you *are* here. What on earth do you have to do with settling Isobel's affairs?"

"Interesting choice of words," Cooper said.

Ken Stephens cleared his throat. "You're both here because you're both mentioned in Isobel's will."

Cooper sat down in the chair next to Hannah's. He was, in her opinion, paying an inordinate amount of attention to preserving the perfect crease in his trousers. "Please don't keep us in suspense. I'm sure Ms. Lowe is panting to know how much she's inherited."

"As long as Isobel didn't do anything idiotic like naming you as a trustee," Hannah snapped, "I don't care what she might have left me."

The disbelief in Cooper's eyes made her long to kick him.

"And why would you be named in her will?" Hannah went on. "It's not as if you were intimate friends. Did you even speak to her when you met in the lobby?"

"Not if I could help it," Cooper said coolly.

"As a matter of fact," Ken Stephens said, "there's no point in anyone getting high hopes. As I just mentioned, Isobel made a will, but after a full month of investigation I've discovered that she actually had very little to leave to anyone."

Hannah frowned. "I don't understand. She owned the condo—"

Ken shook his head. "No. She had a life interest in the condo. With her death, all rights to the Barron's Court property revert to the trust which owns it."

Cooper leaned back in his chair and crossed his arms.

"The furniture," Hannah said. "It must be worth a fortune. Some of it's hundreds of years old."

"Undoubtedly true," Ken agreed. "It was rented from some of the best antique dealers in the city—who, by the way, are a bit anxious to get it all back now that the lease has expired with Isobel's death. Her china and the silver tea service are on loan, too."

"Her jewelry?" Hannah's voice was little more than a breath.

"It's been appraised." Ken Stephens tossed a sheaf of paper on the desk. "Here's a copy of the jeweler's report, but in brief it says that everything Isobel owned was good quality. Extremely good quality—for costume jewelry."

"It was fake?" Hannah whispered.

For a moment the attorney looked almost sympathetic. "I have to admit it fooled me, too, Ms. Lowe." He turned his attention to the folder which lay open on his desk blotter. "Isobel's income consisted of a pension which ends with her death. And she apparently spent the full amount every month, because her bank accounts—checking, savings, and money market—total just under a thousand dollars, which is almost exactly the amount of the bills outstanding at the time of her death. There are no brokerage accounts, no stocks, no money owed to her."

"I hope you're not expecting much in the way of a fee for settling the estate, Stephens." Cooper raised a hand to rub his jaw. "But I guess if you knew Isobel for a while, you should have expected that she'd want something for nothing. How about furs? She had a mink once, and an ermine stole—"

"Now who's taking inventory?" Hannah muttered.

"She got rid of those a few years back," Ken said, "when it became politically incorrect to wear them."

Cooper made a sound which might have been a snort. "More likely it's because they were too heavy to carry around but she didn't want to admit she was getting weak in her declining years."

The attorney shuffled his papers. "Isobel made a provision in her will for the rest of her clothing to be donated to a community theater group."

"A theater?" Cooper asked. "One might almost conclude the woman had a sense of humor after all. In short, it looks as if you get nothing but the towels, Ms. Lowe. Too bad about all your expectations.''

"I didn't have any," Hannah said tightly.

"You can't think I'll believe that. You talk about me taking inventory, but the way you recited that list of possible assets a minute ago, it sounded as if you'd rehearsed it. You've probably been putting yourself to sleep with it every night since Isobel died, counting bonds and jewels and chairs and silver flatware instead of sheep.''

Ignore him, Hannah ordered herself. "About the condo, Mr. Stephens—you did say, after Isobel died, that I could stay on for a while. I'm planning to move, of course, but how long—?''

"I don't see any problem in you staying until all the contents have been moved out. But you know as well as anyone, Ms. Lowe, that condos in Barron's Court are in great demand, and I'm sure the trust would like ·to settle the matter as quickly as possible.''

"I understand." Hannah slid to the edge of her chair. "In that case, I'd better get busy looking for a place to live.''

Ken Stephens extracted a page and closed the folder. "There is just one more thing. In fact, it's actually the most valuable item mentioned in Isobel's will.''

Under any other circumstances, Hannah would have been too preoccupied with her own troubles to notice the way Cooper's muscles tensed. But because she had perched on the edge of her chair, her arm was almost against his, and she could feel the sudden tautness in his body. "In that case," she said dryly, "I think I'll stick around till the bitter end.''

"No one would expect you to do anything else," Cooper agreed.

The senior partner turned his chair so he could reach

into the credenza behind his desk. A moment later, he set a wooden box in the middle of his desk blotter and settled back in his chair.

Cooper's hand went out as if to touch it, and then paused in mid-air as if he was having trouble restraining himself.

Hannah stared at the box in puzzlement. It looked like a small jewelry box, about eight inches square, made of some sort of dark wood which had been heavily carved on every surface she could see. It was pretty enough, she supposed. But what could possibly make it the most valuable thing Isobel had owned?

Not that it has much competition for the honor.

"So what did Isobel say about the box?" Cooper asked.

Was it her imagination, Hannah wondered, or was his voice really just a trifle hoarse?

"Let me get it exactly right." Ken Stephens flipped through the document in front of him. "Here it is. 'I am well aware that Cooper Winston feels the Lovers' Box should be his. But since it is the thing I treasure most, and since it was freely given to me and thus is mine to do with as I choose, I leave it to my young cousin, Hannah Lowe. I hope that for my sake Hannah will take good care of it.'"

Cooper leaped to his feet. "The old biddy! She was obstructionist and opportunistic to the end!"

"The Lovers' Box?" Hannah leaned forward. "Why is it called that?"

"Long story," Cooper said. "I doubt you'd be interested."

Ken Stephens paused, his mouth hanging open, and stared at Cooper. Then he seemed to change his mind about whatever he'd intended to say and pushed the box toward Hannah. "It's yours now, Ms. Lowe."

Hannah's fingers trembled slightly as she picked up the

box. It was heavier than she'd expected, and it felt bulky in her hands. The pattern on top was geometric rather than scenic—she'd half expected to find a picture of a couple portrayed there. But in that case, she supposed, the reason behind the name wouldn't have been a long story.

Hannah pressed the button-like brass knob with her thumb and slowly lifted the lid.

The box was empty, and because the sides and top were quite thick to allow for the depth of the carving, the interior was smaller than she'd expected. The inside of the box didn't even boast a velvet lining; it was only raw wood, sanded smooth—though it was an exotic, fine-grained variety that Hannah didn't recognize. Wasn't there a species called ironwood? The denseness of that type of wood, along with the thickness of the walls, certainly accounted for the box's weight.

But nothing she could see explained why Cooper would be even vaguely interested in owning it.

"That's everything." Ken brushed his hands together as if he was clearing dust off his fingertips. "Ms. Lowe, if you move before all of Isobel's possessions are reclaimed, you'll let me know, I'm sure."

There was no question about the dismissive note in the attorney's voice. Hannah tucked the Lovers' Box under her arm and picked up her handbag.

Cooper was suddenly between her and the door. "Ms. Lowe, I think perhaps if we could talk about this, we could come to an agreement."

Hannah looked up at him, eyes narrowed. "So—now that I have something you want, you'll be nice to me? No, thanks, Mr. Winston. I'm going to go off by myself somewhere and see if I can figure out why this box is so important to you."

She stepped around him to let herself out of the office,

trying to ignore the fact that he was following her so closely she could feel his warmth.

As she opened the door, Ken Stephens said heartily, "No need to hurry away, Winston. I thought my daughter and I would take you to lunch."

From the secretary's desk, Kitty smiled brilliantly. "Do say yes, Mr. Winston. I'd so like to get to know you better."

Hannah rolled her eyes. She was almost disappointed; she'd have expected a little more subtlety from Ken Stephens's daughter. But it was clear there was no need for Hannah to hurry in order to avoid Cooper—he'd be tied up for hours if Kitty had anything to say about it.

Hannah glanced at her watch. She might as well get a sandwich and start looking at the ads for apartments before she went back to work.

Traffic was heavy, and Hannah had to wait for a bus to move before she could cross the street to the deli. Finally, with a whoosh of exhaust, the monster pulled away from the stop, and she darted across.

She was stepping onto the opposite curb when she heard her name called. Surprised, she turned and watched in fascinated disbelief as Cooper dodged between cars—ignoring traffic signals, horns and angry shouts—to follow her.

"You don't have to try to figure it out," he said as he came up to her. "Give me a chance, and I'll tell you why I want that box."

CHAPTER TWO

COOPER felt as if he was shouting in order to be heard above the roaring engine of the bus that had just stopped at the curb, less than three feet away.

Hannah looked thoughtfully at him, and then her gaze slid past him to the bus. For a moment Cooper thought in disbelief that she meant to walk around him and get on it. But just as she sidestepped him, the bus pulled away with a roar and a blast of diesel exhaust.

Relief trickled through him, followed by irritation at the very idea of feeling pleased because she was sticking around to talk to him. As if she didn't have plenty of reason not to rush onto that bus! Her timing was impeccable, though, he had to admit. She'd actually made it look as if she was doing him some sort of favor by staying to listen.

His voice held a sharp edge. "I'd just as soon the rest of the world didn't hear this conversation, so let's go where we won't have to shout. I'll buy you a cup of coffee."

She looked up at him, her green eyes wide and challenging. "Coffee? Aren't you at least going to offer me lunch?"

Cynicism swept over him, and for a split second he considered walking off without a word and leaving her standing there. Then she turned slightly and he caught a glimpse of the Lovers' Box tucked securely under her arm. "I suppose you want to go to the Flamingo Room."

"No," she said pleasantly, "but only because I'm going

27

there tonight. For right now, I'd settle for a hot dog from the stand around the corner. I'm hungry, and it's enough of a sacrifice to actually try to have a conversation with you without attempting to do it on an empty stomach.''

Cooper didn't bother to answer. He thrust out a hand to hail a passing cab and helped Hannah in with chilly politeness. "Cicero's," he told the cabbie.

"Italian? Does that mean you don't like hot dogs?" she asked with obviously feigned interest.

Did she have to look at him that way? Her eyes were not only wide now but so incredibly clear that if he didn't know better he'd think he could see her soul...

Knock it off, Winston, he told himself. He knew from firsthand experience how sharp the woman could be, especially when she was looking innocent. Besides, no relative of Isobel's, especially one that had actually been close enough to live with her, was likely to have a soul any more than the old woman herself had. *And even if she did,* a little voice in the back of his brain murmured, *that wouldn't be the part of Hannah Lowe you'd be interested in, anyway.*

He smothered the thought. Hannah Lowe—attractive? Some men would no doubt think so. Men who didn't know her as well as he did.

What a puritanical sort of name it was, for a woman who was anything but. Her scent, the same sort of musky perfume that Isobel had fancied, gave the lie to that all-American front she tried to put on. Even when she was dressed for a walk with that incredibly bad-tempered dog, she was sexy enough to melt the sidewalk. A hot dog in the park—he almost wished he'd bought her one, just to see what she'd have done with it.

As the maître d' showed them to an alcove at the far side of Cicero's main dining room, Cooper slowed his pace a little, dropping back just far enough to watch the way her silky skirt shimmered as she moved. He'd seen some intriguing walks in his day, but Hannah Lowe's put them all to shame.

Which was exactly what he ought to be feeling right now, he told himself firmly. Shame, for not keeping his mind on the business at hand.

He held back until the maître d' had helped Hannah with her chair, and then he sat down across from her, watching as she placed the Lovers' Box carefully on the corner of the table, as far as possible from him. Which wasn't far, really, because under the narrow table his knee was brushing hers. She didn't pull away, merely looked at him with narrowed eyes.

He gave an order to the waiter and settled back in his chair to watch her fiddle with the Lovers' Box.

Finally it appeared she had it settled to her satisfaction. She looked across at him, and a faint flush crept over her almost-transparent skin. "You look as jumpy as if I was handling dynamite," she said. "What's so special about this box?"

"It's certainly not dangerous. And it wouldn't be anything special to most people. It's important to me only because one of my ancestors was a sea captain who brought it back from an around-the-world voyage close to two centuries ago."

"Sentimental value," she said thoughtfully.

"Exactly." The waiter brought two glasses of red wine and a basket of bread sticks. Cooper pushed the basket invitingly close to her and said abruptly, "I'll give you five hundred dollars for the box, right now."

"Five hundred," she mused. She slowly turned the stem of her wineglass between slim fingers. "I thought you said it was special."

He felt a tinge of reluctant admiration for her negotiating skills. "Don't let Ken Stephens's comments about its value deceive you. On the open market it would bring only a fraction of that. As Isobel knew quite well, the value of that box is precisely what I'm willing to pay for it, and not a dime more."

"But it's so difficult to define sentiment in monetary terms," Hannah said.

"Don't try to blackmail me into a higher offer."

She tilted her head a little to one side. "And don't growl at me. I was simply thinking that it must have every bit as much sentimental value for me as it has for you."

"Because it's the only thing left you by your dear departed aunt? Don't be ridiculous."

She said, sounding almost weary, "She wasn't my aunt, she was my grandfather's cousin."

"Even less of a connection. And less of a reason for you to want to keep it."

"That," Hannah said lightly, "depends entirely on the point of view. Why is it called the Lovers' Box?"

"Agree to sell it to me, and I'll tell you." He watched the light from the sconce above her head play against her hair, bringing out red highlights in the chestnut brown. "How much do you think it's worth?"

"I thought you weren't willing to go above five hundred."

Cooper shrugged. "There are limits on what I'm willing to pay, of course. But humor me, Hannah. Give me an idea of what your estimate is. How much?" *Come on, sweetheart,* he urged. *Once you set a value, no matter how outlandish it is, I've got you. You're committed to making the sale. Then it's just a matter of haggling over the final price.*

"I'll have to think about it," she countered. "Why do you want it so badly?"

He had to admit a reluctant admiration that she'd avoided the trap. "I told you why."

She shook her head. "No. You told me how it got into your family, not why it was so important for you to get it back. Or, for that matter, how it got out of your family and ended up in Isobel's hands. What did she say, in the will? It was freely given to her—something like that. So why you think you deserve to have it back at all is—"

"Nothing was free where Isobel was concerned." Cooper knew he sounded sarcastic. He didn't much care; it was true. "She got that box through deceit and extortion."

Hannah's daintily-arched eyebrows climbed. "Not much of an extortion scheme," she murmured, "if the prize was worth five hundred dollars, tops."

"If that's your way of warning me that you're even better at extortion than Isobel was—"

In a flash, her eyes went from clear to turbulent, from a millpond to a storm-tossed sea. "If you expect me to sit here and listen to you, you'd better be careful about throwing accusations around."

"But if you walk out on me now, you won't get anything at all. If you name a price we can agree on, you'll be that much better off and you won't have to deal with me anymore. So give yourself a break, Hannah. How much do you want for the box?"

"Why are you so sure I'll take money for it? Maybe, if you tell me how Isobel got her hands on it, I'll feel sorry for you and give it back for nothing."

And donkeys will fly, he thought. He hadn't intended to sit around with her long enough to explain it all, but he supposed there was no real reason not to tell her the

Winston side of the story. It might be interesting to find out how it compared to whatever Isobel had told her. "All right, you asked for it. The Captain brought the box home from a trip to the Orient as a gift for his bride, and from then on it was passed down through the generations, given to the oldest child on his or her wedding day."

"The Lovers' Box," she said softly. "Why not call it the Bridal Box?"

"Since I wasn't there when the name originated, I have no idea. At any rate, the box became a sort of talisman, because through all the decades, none of those marriages failed."

"And now I suppose you're planning to get married, so you want it back. That will disappoint Kitty Stephens. You didn't even give her a fair chance—"

"I have no intention of getting married."

"Well, that's a relief."

Cooper eyed her warily. "Why's that?"

"Oh, not because my mind runs along the same channels as Kitty's does," she assured him airily. "It doesn't matter to me whether you get married. But you see, I'd have bet you weren't the superstitious sort who would care about either a trinket or a legend—so it's a relief to know my prophetic abilities haven't gone completely on the fritz. You've left the question unanswered, of course. If you don't want the box for yourself, why is it so important?"

"The Lovers' Box should have gone to my mother on her wedding day. Instead, not long before my parents were married, Isobel persuaded my grandfather to take the name literally and give the box to her instead."

Hannah's eyes weren't stormy anymore, but they were darker than Cooper had ever seen them before—like deep, still pools at the edge of a quiet lake. He could almost feel himself teetering on the shore. A man could drown in those eyes if he wasn't careful.

She was frowning. "I don't quite see—"

"They were lovers," he said grimly.

"Isobel and your grandfather were— *No*."

Cooper nodded. "Paramours. Hanky-panky partners. Cohorts in the horizontal waltz. My grandfather had a sweet tooth, and Isobel was the little cookie he chose to satisfy it. How many ways do I have to say it?"

"*Cookie?* Are you sure you haven't got Isobel mixed up with someone like—oh, Kitty Stephens, say? Isobel was the farthest thing from a *cookie* that I can imagine."

"You're thinking of Isobel at eighty, and I admit it's a little difficult to picture her inspiring a great passion." He paused, and added thoughtfully, "Except perhaps for inciting someone to murder her. She could do that without even trying."

"You didn't, did you?" Hannah sounded suspicious. "Murder her, I mean."

"You surely don't expect me to dignify that with an answer."

"I guess not," she mused. "I probably wouldn't believe you anyway."

"Thanks," Cooper said dryly. "At any rate, to get back to the story... Try to imagine Isobel at—your age, say. What are you? Twenty-seven?"

"Isobel was never my age."

"When she was young, that tongue of hers probably seemed witty instead of sarcastic and callous. She'd have been exotic, slightly shocking—and never boring."

Hannah shook her head, but Cooper thought it was more in resignation than denial.

"And I've seen pictures of her then," he said softly. "If you can look past the crazy fashions and the strange hairstyles, she was really quite beautiful. Enormous eyes, widow's peak, interesting cheekbones…rather like yours, as a matter of fact.''

Cooper didn't realize he'd reached out till his fingertips brushed the hollow of Hannah's cheek. He heard her catch her breath and told himself to stop. But his hand didn't seem to get the message. His fingers slid slowly, barely touching the flesh, along her jawline and down her throat. ''The long neck, the white throat, what they used to call a bee-stung mouth…'' The pad of his thumb tingled as he brushed it ever so softly across her lower lip. ''I can understand why my grandfather lost his head.''

The hell of it was, he really could understand. If Isobel had been half as appealing in her prime as Hannah was…

He watched the rise and fall of Hannah's breasts under the trimly tailored green jacket as she tried to control her breathing, and he knew that his own was just as ragged. What in damnation had he been thinking? This woman wasn't some *cookie*. She was dangerous—even more so, in her own way, than Isobel had been.

He picked up his glass and tossed down the rest of his wine. He could smell the musty scent of her perfume on his hand, as if simply touching her had marked him. ''Anyway, that's how Isobel got the box. Along with a whole lot of other things—the condo, the pension fund…''

''How do you know Isobel demanded all those things? Maybe your grandfather was so besotted with her that he's the one who insisted on setting her up for life.''

''Maybe you're right—about the condo, at least,'' Cooper said deliberately. ''From his point of view, it would have been pretty clever to put the love nest right downstairs from his own place, so he didn't even have to put on an overcoat to go visit his charmer.''

Hannah frowned. ''He lived at Barron's Court, too?''

"In the penthouse I inherited from him. Now that I think about it, perhaps Isobel was the inspiration for his whole scheme to turn the old Barron's Hotel into condos in the first place. Before that, my grandparents lived in one of the big old mansions south of Grand Avenue—and he could hardly have installed Isobel in the guest room without Gran noticing. But we're drifting from the point."

"The Lovers' Box." Hannah touched it with a fingertip.

"I want the box so I can put it back where it belongs, Hannah—in my mother's hands. I'm willing to pay good money for it, just as I was willing to pay Isobel."

"Oh, really?" Skepticism dripped from Hannah's voice. "Then—if Isobel was so mercenary—why didn't she sell it to you?"

He'd thought until then that he was making progress. She'd been softening, he was sure of it, until he'd gotten careless and made a misstep. What was wrong with him, to make him forget that she was a demon of a negotiator?

"Because it wasn't a matter of money to her, by then," he said irritably. He knew even as he said it that he was handing Hannah a weapon. But he couldn't seem to stop himself; once he'd opened the wound his pain seemed to overflow.

"She liked the feeling of power she got from keeping me dangling," he went on bitterly. "She liked knowing that even though my grandfather had been dead for years, she could still remind his family that she hadn't gone away. She liked being a thorn in the flesh—cashing her pension check every month, still living just one floor down from the family home, running into me in the elevator from time to time and politely asking how I was doing, as if she were an old friend of the family. And she liked keeping that box where she could look at it now and then and smile."

And what about you, Hannah? he asked himself. *Are you going to be just like her? Are you going to use all that against me?*

"I'm sorry," Hannah said. "I imagine Isobel was always like that. But whatever she did really has nothing to do with me." She toyed with her wineglass and said casually, "So how much did you offer her for the box?"

He stared at her for a long moment. Well, he thought, he had his answer. She was going to hold him up for everything she could get. "Surely you don't think I'm going to tell you."

"You mean you won't pay me as much as you'd have given her?" She shook her head sadly.

"I'm sure as hell not going to make you a free gift of the information." His voice was hard-edged. "At least you'll have to do that much on your own. Isobel did everything else for you. Not only did she give you the box, but she handed you complete instructions on how to bargain with it. She made sure, from the way she wrote her will, that you'd know it was worth more than anything else she could leave you. And by dangling my name, she told you precisely how to cash in on it." Cooper snapped a bread stick in half. "So I suppose the only question remaining now is how much you're like her."

"What?"

"It's quite apparent you've inherited Isobel's sadistic nature," he said deliberately. "The unknown is whether you've developed it into a fine art, as she did. How much am I going to have to pay to get back what's mine?"

Hannah stared at him. Cooper put the bread stick between his lips like a cigar and waited to see if the strategy would work. Whatever figure she named, of course, he had no intention of paying it. But once she'd set a price, no matter how outrageous, he could force her into a final compromise. Asking leading questions hadn't succeeded in getting her to name an amount; would goading her to fury work any better?

"Nothing."

Her voice was so quiet that he almost thought he'd heard wrong. "What did you say?"

"I mean no amount of money would be enough," she said. "You're not getting the box—no matter what." She fumbled in her bag and tossed a handful of cash onto the table. "That should cover my half of the bill." She stood, picked up the Lovers' Box, and stepped away from the table. Then she turned toward him again. "One more thing, Mr. Winston. Since I've just paid for a glass of wine that I never intended to drink, I might as well get some good out of it."

She picked up her still-full glass and with one smooth and efficient turn of her wrist threw the contents at him.

He saw it coming as if in slow motion, first a few droplets and then a tidal wave of red wine, and he closed his eyes against the onslaught. But she hadn't aimed at his face; the liquid sloshed across the breadth of his chest instead, soaking his favorite tie, the front of his once-white shirt, the lapels of his charcoal suit.

"Excuse me," Hannah said to the waiter, who had rushed forward, his tray of hors d'oeuvres still balanced, to fumble with a napkin. "I do hope I didn't get any on the carpet."

Then she walked away, head high, spine straight, with the Lover's Box held firmly in both hands, leaving only silence in her wake.

The breeze had picked up, whipping through the canyons of downtown. But Hannah was steaming, too agitated to sit still, so instead of hailing a cab she walked all the way back downtown to Stephens & Webster.

Cooper Winston had deserved every last drop, she told herself. The moment when it was apparent he'd seen the deluge coming and knew he couldn't do a thing to prevent it would be part of Hannah's scrapbook of precious memories for the rest of her life. It was just too bad it had been only a glass of wine, and a small one at that; if he'd ordered the bottle, she'd have smashed it over his head.

Of course, she admitted, there was the little matter of effectively squashing any faint possibility that he might consider taking his legal business to Stephens & Webster. And if he were to complain about her conduct to Ken Stephens...

"He still deserved it," Hannah muttered unrepentantly.

Besides, when she thought about it, she decided that he was unlikely to say anything to anybody about the incident. He'd look like a fool if he told that story—and if there was one thing she was certain of about Cooper, it was that he didn't like looking silly. Experienced businessman that he was, he would never admit that he'd been outmaneuvered in a straightforward business proposition by a young woman whose law school diploma was practically still warm from the press, much less that Hannah's final counteroffer had been a glass of wine.

No, his revenge would be of a different sort. And she was fairly sure there would be consequences of her actions—even though the whole thing had been his fault in the first place. If he hadn't leaped to unwarranted assumptions about her, Hannah wouldn't have lost her temper at all.

So what if Isobel hadn't been any plaster saint? That wasn't exactly a news flash, though Hannah still had a little trouble picturing her elderly cousin as a courtesan extraor-

dinaire. Fluffy, agreeable, and charming weren't words
that sprang to mind where Isobel was concerned.

But then, what made Hannah assume that she knew the
criteria for being a good mistress? Maybe fluffy, agreeable,
and charming were precisely what men like Cooper's
grandfather *weren't* looking for.

Still, whatever Isobel's history, it didn't mean that the
inclination for extortion and blackmail ran through the rest
of the family, as Cooper so clearly believed.

He'd been remembering his fifteen million dollars, of
course. But though Hannah admitted that her timing could
have been a lot more convenient, there had been nothing
shady about her actions in the restaurant chain deal. She'd
simply discovered, at the very last minute, a loophole that
everyone else had overlooked altogether.

What really annoyed her about the Lovers' Box was the
fact that right up till the last minute she'd actually been
feeling sympathetic. She'd been almost ready to wipe away
a tear as she handed his treasure back to him. The last
foolish question she'd asked had been prompted more by
curiosity than anything else; she'd been not only wondering exactly how much the box was worth to him, but she'd
been toying with the idea of how grateful he'd be when
she told him he didn't have to pay her anything at all…

Not far from the law office, on a sudden whim, she
stopped to take a closer look at Cooper's treasure.

In strong sunlight, the Lovers' Box looked even less
likely as an object of obsession. It was pretty enough, but
on close inspection she could see a basic crudity about the
carving and a certain lack of grace in the proportions of
the box. One thing was certain; Cooper had been right
when he said that no one else would pay as much for it
as he was willing to do.

You probably should have grabbed the five hundred

bucks and run, Hannah thought wryly. But no, she'd had to probe for the whole story. What on earth had she been thinking of?

And what was she going to do now?

Perhaps more important, what would Cooper do? He was momentarily stymied, but Hannah didn't expect that state of affairs to last long. In fact, she wouldn't be surprised if he'd thought out another plan by the time he'd changed his shirt.

But what would he try next? Persuasion? Threats? Outright burglary?

She'd have to deal with those things when and if they came up. In the meantime, she decided, there were a few basic measures she could take in the name of self-protection.

As soon as she'd stashed the Lovers' Box in a hiding place that she hoped was safely out of Cooper's reach, she dusted one problem from her hands. But there was still Brenton Bannister to consider. Brenton, and his promise of a very special evening. One, he had seemed to imply, which would change the rest of Hannah's life.

The uneasy flutter she'd felt in the pit of her stomach when he'd issued the invitation came back again, even more strongly.

Hannah was in the law library, still poring over Jacob Jones's files, when Brenton came in. "What's keeping you?" he said. "I've been waiting."

Hannah stopped fitting together the bits of an invoice which had crumbled with age. "You said you had clients all afternoon. I told your secretary I'd be here if you needed me."

"Very discreet of you to put it that way." He chuckled. "I always knew you had sense, Hannah. She said you were very bright-eyed when you came in, and that you looked as if you'd had quite a surprise.''

''I suppose you could put it that way.'' Hannah fitted the last piece of the invoice into place, glanced at it, concluded that the information it contained carried no importance to the legal matter at hand, and put it in the finished stack.

''So tell me the good news. How did you and Ken Stephens get along? And when will Isobel's estate all be wrapped up?''

''Oh, it's pretty well finished already,'' Hannah said dryly. ''All but the dust settling.''

''I was right, wasn't I?'' Brenton pushed aside a stack of papers and sat down on the corner of the table. ''She left you everything she owned.''

''Just about.''

''What did I tell you?'' Satisfaction almost dripped from his voice. ''You can give me all the details over a nice long dinner.''

Hannah brushed off her hands and stood up. As she fitted the lid back on the box, she said casually, ''You were absolutely right, Brenton. The only trouble with your scenario is that Isobel cut it right down to the wire and died without a penny to her name. So I was right, too—because in fact she didn't leave me anything at all.''

She'd taken two steps toward the door before she realized that Brenton hadn't moved, except for his mouth dropping open.

That was pretty much the identical reaction she'd had, of course. Not inheriting hadn't surprised her—but the fact that there was nothing to inherit had been a stunner.

''Nothing?'' Brenton's voice was almost a croak. ''But...but she was a wealthy woman!''

''She appeared to be a wealthy woman,'' Hannah corrected. "In fact, she was something of an expert at appearing to be well-off." She succinctly repeated Ken Stephens's rundown regarding Isobel's condo, furniture, jewelry, china, silver, and furs.

She was just starting to tell Brenton about the odd little Lovers' Box when she realized that would lead almost inevitably to telling him about the scene at Cicero's.

Brenton seemed too shocked to notice that her story had abruptly broken off. "Nothing," he repeated. "She left you nothing at all?"

Hannah's eyes narrowed. "Exactly why is that so important?"

"Oh, I just…" His voice was little more than a whisper. "I was so certain. At least, she always seemed to indicate that you'd get everything she owned."

"I did. She just didn't own much of anything."

"But it was like she *told* me that you would—" He broke off.

Hannah braced her hands on the table. "You seriously thought I was going to be rich, didn't you?"

He didn't answer, but his gaze shifted uneasily away.

And you were planning to end up with a good share of my supposed wealth, weren't you? Now she understood. That was why Brenton had invited her out tonight, after months of casual friendliness. That was why he'd trotted out the line about getting to know her, and that was why he'd left it dangling instead of going on to tell her how special she was, and how important she'd become to him. He'd left it to Hannah to fill in the blank, and she'd done exactly as he'd expected she would.

Now she could see precisely how careful he'd been to say nothing that could be taken as a commitment. Nothing that he couldn't escape. Even that invitation to dinner had been very carefully phrased….

Hannah kept her voice level. "Are we still going out tonight, Brenton?"

She didn't quite know what she'd do if he said yes, for she'd rather share a meal with a rattlesnake. But she suspected that Brenton was so eager to escape that he wouldn't stop to consider the possibility she was bluffing.

"Actually..." His voice almost rasped. "You don't feel like celebrating, I'm sure, under the circumstances. So maybe it would be better if we didn't."

How thoughtful it was of him, Hannah mused, to put her feelings first! "Then how about taking me out for a nice dinner to commiserate?" she asked gently.

He swallowed hard. He looked, she thought, like a hunted rabbit. "The Jones case," he said. "I really do need to burn the midnight oil on it, so—"

"And of course it would be foolish to spend money on me at the Flamingo Room if there's no chance of getting it back."

She could see the truth written in his face.

Too annoyed to think it through, Hannah said, "If I'd told you Isobel had left me a million or two, would you have proposed to me tonight, Brenton? Or would you have waited till you could check out the facts with Ken Stephens, just to be certain I was telling the truth?"

She stopped there, but only by biting her tongue hard. No matter how much he deserved it, she couldn't tell him to jump off a cliff; he was still her boss.

And it was suddenly and perfectly clear to Hannah that not only was Brenton Bannister a jerk, but he was the kind of animal who became most dangerous when cornered. Almost accidentally, she'd done precisely that, by forcing him to admit—if only by a look—what he had plotted.

She'd been concerned about what kind of revenge

Cooper might take on her—but she was terrified of what Brenton might do.

She was an embarrassment to him now, that was clear. Perhaps he even saw her as a threat, able to damage his career by telling this story. And in Brenton Bannister's narrow view of the world, whether she was an embarrassment or an active danger, the answer was obviously the same: Hannah would have to go.

He would stay within the rules, for he was too clever to break them and give her cause to charge him with sexual harassment or discrimination. But one way or another, he'd get rid of her—and soon.

Unless she did something to prevent it.

But what could she possibly do?

She forced herself to smile at him. "You're right," she said. "It's just as well we're not going out. We've both got work to do to have the Jones case ready for trial. In fact, I'm going to take a box of papers home with me now. But first, I want to thank you, Brenton. It *has* been a very special evening."

And, she thought wryly, it had certainly turned out to be one which would change the rest of her life.

CHAPTER THREE

By THE time Hannah got halfway back to Barron's Court, she was regretting the impulse which had made her seize a carton of Jacob Jones's papers. She'd done it only as a sort of bluff—so that Brenton wouldn't be able to accuse her of walking out on undone tasks—rather than because she had any real intention of working tonight; with her mind going in circles, she'd be too afraid of missing something important.

But as she walked the few blocks from the law firm to Barron's Court, the box had grown as heavy as the weight that seemed to have descended on her shoulders. She propped the carton on a corner of a small table in the lobby, glad of a moment's relief, while she waited for the elevator.

How much different things looked than they had early in the morning, she thought, when she and Brutus had stood right here, fresh from a walk and feeling great. In one day, she'd near-as-nothing lost both her home and her job....

And Cooper Winston would no doubt add, with a note of glee in his voice, that she'd lost her expectations, as well. He probably thought the only reason she'd come to visit Isobel in the first place had been to look over her circumstances and decide if the old woman was worthwhile prey!

Impatiently, Hannah pushed the button again. The way her luck was running, the elevator had probably broken down. At least, the lighted dial above the polished Art

45

Deco doors said that the darned thing hadn't moved off seven since she'd come in.

All she wanted to do was get upstairs, fix herself a cup of tea, climb into her bed, and pull the comforter over her head while she waited for a new day to dawn. Whatever happened tomorrow, she told herself, it couldn't possibly be as bad as today had been.

She was bracing herself for the climb up the long flights of stairs—and wishing even more that she'd left the carton of papers in the law library—when the elevator finally began to move. "And there's absolutely no doubt," she muttered, "the way my day has been going, who is going to get off when it gets to the lobby." It was like the man had radar, knowing precisely when and where he was least wanted.

She stepped to the side as the door opened. To her surprise, however, instead of Cooper, the occupant was a jeans-clad workman who was straining to carry a thick slab of dark-stained wood which was nearly as broad as his outstretched arms. He nodded to Hannah as he maneuvered the slab out into the lobby, then stopped just a few steps away to readjust the padding which had started to slip away from the wood.

She said, "It would be easier to move something that size on the service elevator. You do know Barron's Court has a service elevator? It allows this one to be left free for the residents to use."

"Yeah, I know." The workman's tone was breezy; he was obviously unperturbed by the irony in Hannah's voice. "We're using that one, too. Got a whole apartment to clean out, and we need to be done before the old people who live here start going to bed." The protective padding dropped to the floor, and he called to another workman, "Hey, Joe, give me a hand to wrap this up again."

A whole apartment to clean out? Hannah's head started to ache. No wonder the elevator seemed to have been stuck on the seventh floor; that was Isobel's floor.

And, with the concealing padding out of the way, Hannah didn't have to look twice at the carved surface of the slab to know that it was the headboard of her bed that the workman was carrying out. Or, to put it more accurately, the one she'd been using—the elaborate tester bed which had been the centerpiece of Isobel's guest room. It no more belonged to Hannah than it had to Isobel.

Ken Stephens had said that the antique dealers were anxious to have their property back, but Hannah had assumed that it would take a few days at least for them to make arrangements to move everything. Obviously she'd been wrong.

She stepped onto the elevator, steeling herself for what she was likely to see on the seventh floor.

The door of Isobel's condo stood open, and a sideboard half blocked the hallway, but the scene wasn't as confused or noisy as Hannah had expected.

Dead center in the living room, a flustered Kitty Stephens stood holding a clipboard full of papers, while a man looked over her shoulder and pointed at something. "It's right there on the list," he said. "The Pembroke table. See it?"

"But there are tables everywhere," Kitty said helplessly. "How should I know which one that is?"

Hannah moved across the room, set her carton down in a corner behind the door, and lifted the last issue of Isobel's favorite glamour magazine off the polished surface of a small side table. "It's this one," she said. "Be careful with it, because it should probably be in a museum."

The man eyed Hannah with a tinge of respect. "Don't

worry about how we'll treat it. As a matter of fact, there's a museum waiting for it.''

Hannah wondered if Isobel had known that, and decided dispassionately that if the museum or the dealer had actively tried to get the table away from her, the attempt probably would have only increased both Isobel's appreciation of her treasure and her determination to hang on to it as long as possible.

Just as she had enjoyed keeping the Lovers' Box away from Cooper....

You don't know that, Hannah reminded herself. *You've only got his word for the whole story.*

Without a doubt, however, there had been a note of pleasure in that brief passage from Isobel's will, a sort of gleeful delight which had come through despite Ken Stephens's dry and scholarly tone...

Relief flooded Kitty's face. She held out the clipboard to Hannah. ''Now that you're here, Ms. Lowe, you can take over. Daddy gave me this list and told me to come and supervise, but how should I know what they're supposed to leave?''

''Except for the box I just brought in and the clothes in the back bedroom, not much,'' Hannah said. ''And since the man appears to know his job, I'm going to let him do it, Kitty. I'd suggest you do the same.'' She stood aside to let a workman pass, then headed toward the kitchen.

The dining room, she saw, had already been denuded of Isobel's Waterford crystal and Haviland china. On the walls, only discolored shadows marked the place where paintings and prints had hung.

Art, Hannah thought with a mental snap of the fingers. Ken Stephens hadn't singled it out as he listed Isobel's possessions, but obviously the art collection had been on loan, too. The old woman had no doubt made a deal with a gallery somewhere along the way.

Just as she had dealt with Hannah—giving her a room in the most exclusive condo complex in the city in exchange for service as an unofficial social secretary.

Shortly after she'd moved into the condo, when Hannah had begun to realize that Isobel had an ulterior motive in inviting her, she'd been almost amused by the old woman's shrewdness. Now that she saw the pattern, however, it didn't seem so funny anymore. No doubt about it; Isobel had been a genius at getting what she wanted without spending a cent for it.

In the kitchen, Isobel's decorative Wedgwood plates were gone from their hangers above the cabinets, but otherwise everything looked pretty much the same. Hannah plugged the kettle in and sat down at the breakfast bar to wait for the water to boil. They could take away her bed and even the comforter she'd been half planning to pull over her head, but at least she could still have her tea.

This had turned out to be a prize-winner of a day, she mused. And it was a very memorable evening, as well, if not quite in the sense she'd originally anticipated.

She'd expected it would be difficult, a challenge to all her skills, to keep Brenton as her friend and preserve their good working relationship while gently but firmly depressing his hopes that she would return his love...

What a hoot that had turned out to be!

Hannah could still hardly believe that Brenton had actually thought he was such an irresistible stud that all he had to do was crook a finger and she'd fall into his arms. Surely she had never given him reason to think anything of the sort.

He was attractive enough, though she felt like a fool

now for having been deceived at all—even if she had found him appealing only as a friend, not a lover.

But perhaps she was being too hard on herself. There was no question that Brenton was a master at playing up to a woman, charming her and intriguing her, without ever passing the point of no return. Hannah could see now how he'd even courted her, not with the usual methods of flowers and dates but with something much more subtle, and much more appealing to Hannah—challenging and stimulating conversation. He had appealed to her intellect, asking for her advice and insights. And she had fallen for it.

He'd done the same sort of thing with Isobel, she remembered, on several occasions when the older woman had stopped by Hannah's cubicle after a visit with Ken Stephens. The basic technique had been the same, though the expression was different. With Isobel, Brenton had been teasing, flattering, and ever-so-slightly flirtatious.

At the time, Hannah had thought he was being very considerate in putting his own work aside, and encouraging Hannah to do the same, in order to entertain an elderly, lonely woman. But as she looked back, the episodes had a much more sinister twist. He'd been impressing Isobel with what a charmer he was. And he'd been implying to Isobel with every gesture what he would never have said openly to Hannah—that he intended to marry her…

Was that why Isobel had wanted Hannah to have the Lovers' Box—because she'd recognized that Brenton was courting her? Because it was the only thing she could leave, and she had wanted to signal her approval?

Hannah could see plainly how Brenton had played them both. She herself had reacted like a fish on a line, so predictable that it made her feel ill to think about it. She'd even thanked him for his helpfulness in intervening with

Ken Stephens to arrange for her to stay in the condo after Isobel's death...

Helpful. It was apparent now, of course, that Brenton hadn't been trying to help her but himself—by using the excuse of the condo in order to feel out the situation, to find out if Hannah really was the heiress he expected her to be. Obviously Ken Stephens had played his cards very close to his chest, though, for Brenton had come away with the wrong impression.

At the moment, however, none of that mattered. The important question was what Hannah was going to do next.

She could tell her story, of course. She could go up the corporate ladder to Brenton's boss, or—since she now had a more than passing acquaintance with Ken Stephens—she could go straight to the senior partner.

But there were a couple of problems with that plan of action. The first was whether she'd even be believed. Not likely, Hannah thought dispassionately. It would be her word against Brenton's—that of a seasoned junior partner against an associate who had been with the firm less than a year.

And even if she overcame that obstacle, there was the question of what action she could reasonably expect the firm to take. For what, after all, had Brenton Bannister really done? He was certainly a jerk, but that wasn't a crime.

For that matter, she reflected, she'd have a difficult time proving—at least with the kind of evidence that lawyers respected—that he was a jerk. All he'd actually done was to invite her out to dinner and then cancel.

She'd be willing to bet that he'd been carrying a diamond ring in his pocket tonight and that he'd had every intention of using it, along with whatever lies and deception he could think of, in order to get what he wanted.

She'd also bet that if he had proposed and she'd accepted, he would have rushed her off to a judge to marry her in the shortest possible time—before she could have second thoughts.

But Hannah's hunches weren't evidence, either. She couldn't even swear that he'd lied to her, or made false promises—because in fact he hadn't said anything definite at all.

No. The only thing she could accomplish by telling her story to Brenton's superiors was to make herself look like a fool. Or even worse, like a manipulative shrew who had thought up the whole accusation in an effort to get back at him for *not* fancying her.

The way he'd helped her—the brand-new associate— through her challenging first months at Stephens & Webster would add to his credibility, not hers. In fact, when it came right down to the bottom line, Brenton had been a textbook model of the perfect boss. There had never been a suggestion of undue pressure, or a suspicion of sexual harassment. He'd never even told an off-color story in Hannah's hearing, much less made any kind of open threat. Even tonight, only the hardness in his eyes had hinted that her job was at stake—and she knew he could convincingly deny any intention of getting rid of her.

Yet Hannah was as certain of her doom as if a guillotine blade were hanging over her.

The water boiled, and she got a tea bag from the canister and reached for a cup from the cupboard shelf only to find that there were none.

Of course, she thought. Isobel's everyday dishes had been Spode china. To add to the difficulty, there probably wasn't a spoon left to stir her tea even if she'd been able to brew it. Only now did she remember Isobel declaring that stainless steel flatware left a horrid aftertaste which sterling silver didn't. And if Isobel's flatware had been silver, Hannah knew, there was one sure thing about it— it hadn't belonged to Isobel.

Hannah poured the boiling water down the drain.

So what was she going to do? What *could* she do? Quit before Brenton found an excuse to fire her? Try to get a transfer into another section of the firm?

She thought about it for a long time. Then, with a sigh, she climbed the stairs to the penthouse.

Cooper spent the afternoon in his office, but nobody could say he accomplished much while he was there.

It was without a doubt true that even on a good day, he'd have had trouble keeping his mind on the preliminary draft of the company's annual financial report, with its painstaking and seemingly endless summary of acquisitions and divestitures, balance sheets and dividends. But after the scene Hannah had treated him to at Cicero's, a dry-as-dust financial report was the last thing which could have held his attention.

Bar graphs and pie charts had no power to mesmerize him when a pair of stormy green eyes kept appearing between him and the page. Unadorned summaries of profits and losses couldn't compete with the memory of a low, almost sultry voice saying, *Since I've just paid for a glass of wine that I never intended to drink, I might as well get some good out of it.*

He had to give Hannah credit, though. That trick had been worthy of Isobel in her prime—and he'd heard some tales about Isobel through the years, whether he'd wanted to or not.

Some of his grandfather's old cronies were still around, and Cooper had run into most of them in the years he'd spent on the board of the family's charitable foundation, which the old man had set up long ago. They liked reliving the glorious days of their youth. "And probably exaggerating them, too," he told himself. Still, even greatly-inflated memories were generally built on a kernel of truth.

So Cooper had listened to whatever they wanted to tell him, because that was a small price to pay in return for the sizable checks they were in the habit of writing to the foundation. He must have heard all the stories by now. And there was no doubt in his mind that Isobel Lowe had called the tune and his grandfather had danced to it.

What had the old man seen in that woman to make him act like such a fool?

The question brought its own answer. *You know very well what the attraction was,* Cooper told himself. Absolute raw sex appeal—he'd felt the tug of it himself this afternoon, despite the fact that his previous experience with her had told him that messing with Hannah Lowe was a perilous proposition.

Fortunately, his well-honed sense of self-preservation had kicked in just in time. Still, the knowledge that he had been tempted had left him even more determined to get the Lovers' Box away from Hannah.

And he wouldn't pay for the privilege, either, he told himself. She didn't know it yet, but she'd missed her only chance to cash in.

He didn't know exactly how he was going to go about it, but he was certain of one thing. He would end up with the Lovers' Box—and Hannah would have nothing to show for it.

To reach the fire stairs leading to the penthouse floor, Hannah had to first dodge the workmen who were carrying an enormous armoire out of Isobel's bedroom. The work was going fast; she guessed that in another half hour all the major pieces would be gone.

There was no sign of Kitty Stephens as Hannah walked through the condo, and the man who'd been arguing with her about the inventory was now in possession of the clipboard. ''The clothes in the back bedroom, Miss,'' he said as Hannah passed. ''I hope you don't mind, but we just stacked them in piles on the floor. There was nowhere else to put them.''

Hannah nodded and ducked around the end of the fainting couch where Isobel had lain to read magazines and eat chocolates on the rare afternoons when she wasn't playing bridge. Now it looked forlorn, sitting at an awkward angle in the foyer with its cushions askew, waiting to be carried away.

Things are getting pretty bad, she mocked herself, *when you start feeling sorry for the furniture!*

She'd never gone to the top floor of Barron's Court before. She'd never even been tempted to take a peek. She'd done her best—futile as the effort had been—to stay out of Cooper's way.

But one couldn't live long in Barron's Court without learning a little about the layout and the history of the place. How Cooper's grandfather had foreseen a trend of multi-unit housing which was aimed not at young people who couldn't yet afford a single-family house, but at the wealthy who didn't want to be bothered with the upkeep on one. How the old man—or perhaps he hadn't been so old at the time—had bought the elegant but tattered Barron's Hotel and turned it into the most exclusive living spaces in the city. And how he'd reserved the entire top floor for his own family—the penthouse which Cooper had inherited.

Hannah wondered how the love nest one floor down had

managed to escape the legend, for the story Cooper had
told her this afternoon had all the elements that gossips
loved. Was it really not common knowledge? Or had the
tenants' respect for the betrayed wife kept the talk hushed?
Or perhaps even a healthy wariness of Isobel herself?

Hannah pushed open the fire door at the top of the stairs
and emerged into a small lobby exactly like the ones on
the other seven floors. She was vaguely disappointed,
though she didn't quite know what she'd expected. Walls
covered in gold leaf, perhaps?

As on the other floors, the stairs had emerged next to
the service elevator instead of the public one, so she
walked around to the front side of the lobby, where an
elegant pediment-topped door beckoned. She took a deep
breath—probably the last one she'd be able to manage for
a while, she thought wryly—and rang the bell.

There was nothing but quiet from inside. And why
should she be surprised at that, Hannah asked herself. Just
because she'd decided it was necessary for her to see
Cooper didn't mean he'd be home waiting for her—

The door swung silently open, and Cooper, tall and
broad-shouldered in a dark sweater and jeans, raised an
inquisitive eyebrow at her.

She felt very small, standing there face-to-face with him.
She hadn't felt this tongue-tied since the first time she'd
stood in a real courtroom, in front of a real judge. And
that had been a simple matter, nothing more than routine
paperwork. This, on the other hand…

She swallowed hard. "I'd like to talk to you, if you have
a few minutes."

Slowly, Cooper's gaze traveled over her from head to
foot and back. Then he stepped away from the door and
with the smallest of gestures, invited her in.

She'd known that the place must be huge, because each

of the lower floors contained at least four spacious apartments and some as many as eight. But she had been unprepared for marble columns supporting a vaulted ceiling over a stone-floored foyer large enough to house a costume ball.

Beyond the foyer lay a large living room, darkened except for the twinkle of gold at the windows provided by the spread-out lights of the city below. Off to one side of the foyer was a formal dining room with a table that would seat at least eighteen. The corners were in shadow, the room lit only by a portrait light above an Impressionist painting on the far wall.

"You're too late," Cooper said coolly. "It was last year that my mother turned the place into a decorator's showcase to benefit the family foundation. But next time I decide to open the place for tours as a fund-raiser, I'll be sure to let you know so you can buy a ticket."

"Was I staring?" Hannah tapped her toe on the stone floor. "I'm sorry, I've just never seen the contents of an entire marble quarry put to use in one room before."

For a moment she thought he was going to throw her out right then. Instead, he pointed down a hallway between the dining and living rooms, toward an open door, and Hannah followed the wordless command.

She heard the murmur of voices from the room and held back for a moment. If he had company...

"I was watching football," he said impatiently. "And believe me, if the score was close, I'd tell you to sit down and shut up till the game was over." He pushed the door wide and ushered her into a large den.

This, Hannah thought, was obviously the room where he spent most of his time. On the coffee table was the television remote control, the morning newspaper, a briefcase which spilled papers, and a king-size bowl of popcorn.

Until that moment, Hannah had forgotten that she hadn't bothered to eat either lunch or dinner. Once reminded, however, her stomach wasn't about to let her ignore the oversight.

Cooper waved her to the couch and shut off the television set. "What do you want, Hannah?"

"Right now," Hannah said honestly, "that popcorn."

"The chef at the Flamingo Room will be very disappointed to hear there was nothing on the menu that satisfied you." He pushed the bowl toward her.

"I didn't go after all."

She took a handful. The popcorn was still steaming hot, and it was delicious.

"At least if you toss this at me it won't cause permanent damage," Cooper mused.

Hannah picked through her popcorn and selected a kernel so she didn't have to look at him. "I shouldn't have thrown the wine."

Cooper sat down on the other end of the couch, half turned to face her, with his long legs sprawling. "Is that an apology or an opening gambit? Not that it matters much, I'm just curious."

"I'll pay the cleaning bill."

"You can't seriously think there's any point in sending a white silk shirt to the dry cleaner after it's been soaked in red wine."

"That was silk? Then I guess you're right."

"But since you insist," he added smoothly, "I'll certainly send you the bill for replacing it. Now, if that's what you came up here for—"

"Actually," Hannah said, "I have a sort of proposition for you. About the Lovers' Box."

Cooper's voice was dry. "I thought that might be it. Perhaps I should warn you up front that I'm not willing to pay nearly as much as I was earlier today."

She leaned forward and lined half a dozen fat popcorn kernels up along the edge of the coffee table. "It isn't exactly money that I have in mind."

The silence drew out until Hannah couldn't stand it any longer. She stole a look at him through her lashes. He was absolutely still. Like a predator who was lying in wait for the perfect instant to pounce, she thought with trepidation.

"Now that," Cooper drawled, "could be very interesting indeed."

He watched in fascination as Hannah jerked upright, as if he'd jabbed her with a red-hot poker. "Wait just a minute," she snapped. "If you think that I'm offering to trade the Lovers' Box for a roll in the hay with you—"

"Maybe you're not just thinking of one," Cooper said thoughtfully.

She bristled. "You might remember that I'm the one who has something you want."

Several things, in fact. Cooper squashed the thought. Now was not the time to let himself be distracted by the delightful way her indignant intake of breath had affected her figure. "You're the one who said this was a proposition."

"I didn't mean that kind!"

"So tell me what you did mean. There's obviously something you want in return, or you wouldn't be sitting here trying to negotiate."

She fiddled with the row of popcorn kernels. "How would you like to have the Lovers' Box back without paying a cent for it?"

He'd agree to that about the same time he'd invest in

the Brooklyn Bridge. "Nothing's free, Hannah." Cooper scooped up a handful of popcorn and, one by one, tossed each kernel into the air to catch it on his tongue. "So let's stop playing games. What is it you want?"

He was obscurely pleased that she finally looked directly at him. "First, I want to make it painfully clear that what I am proposing is to be for appearance's sake only. Nothing more. I am not interested in being your…cookie, wasn't that the word you used?"

"Nobody asked you to be," Cooper said coolly. "A roll in the hay, as you so elegantly phrased it—"

She blushed again.

"Or even several of them, is not the same thing as a long-standing arrangement."

"I beg your pardon for not understanding the fine details, but in my book, there's no important difference at all. They're equally distasteful. So it doesn't matter whether you're talking about a one-night stand or a full-fledged affair, I'm not interested. Is that perfectly understood?"

"And I'm not planning to repeat the mistakes my grandfather made," Cooper said. "But it would have been very ungentlemanly of me to point out, before you made yourself clear, that I'm not interested in either a one-night stand or a full-fledged affair. However, now I'm absolutely panting to hear what you *are* negotiating for—if it's not your lovely self."

Suddenly she seemed very interested in the cover of a report which lay on the coffee table. "I want you to pretend to be interested in me. Seriously interested."

Cooper gave a soundless whistle. "You must think I'm an idiot. I'd be setting myself up for a breach of promise suit."

"Of course not. I mean, I don't think you're an idiot—"

"I don't suppose you'd put that in writing."

"—and I have no intention of suing you. I couldn't, anyway," Hannah pointed out, "unless there was something concrete to prove you'd made a promise in the first place—an engagement ring or something. Besides, I don't mean anything *that* serious. Just…oh, be my date for the bar association banquet in a couple of weeks. Pick me up at the office a few times. Act a bit protective—maybe even possessive. That's all."

"Why?" Cooper asked baldly.

She obviously didn't want to answer, for she hesitated before saying, "Because I've run into a little trouble at work."

"A little trouble? I'm betting that your definition doesn't come close to matching mine."

"I've…" She sighed. "Let's just say I've run afoul of my boss, and as of this evening it's a race to see if he can find an excuse to fire me before I can find another job. But if I was dating you, he wouldn't dare fire me."

"I don't see why he wouldn't. I don't pull a lot of weight around Stephens & Webster."

"But you could if you wanted to. The firm—and especially Brenton—wants you as a client."

"And you're the bait who's going to draw me in."

"Of course not. I mean, not really. But if he thought that I *could* bring your business into the firm, Brenton wouldn't dare even to make my life miserable, much less fire me. With you behind me, I could buy a little time to look around for another position."

"How much time do you have in mind?"

"I don't know, exactly. As long as it takes to get a decent offer from another firm."

Did she really think he was crazy enough to sign on for

an open-ended commitment? "You could just quit, and look for a new job at your leisure."

"I can't go a month or two without a paycheck. You have no idea how much debt I'm carrying because of law school. Besides, any businessman knows perfectly well that it's easier to get a new job when you already have one."

"It's true that you're more appealing to an employer if you don't look desperate," Cooper agreed.

"And if I left a firm like Stephens & Webster—after less than a year on the job—without having another offer first, I'd look very desperate. I must stay on, because it's a matter of professional survival. So you see—"

"What I see," Cooper interrupted, "is no earthly reason why I should interfere."

"The Lovers' Box," she reminded, as if she were bribing a reluctant toddler.

"I want it back, yes. But I'm not sure I want it badly enough to put myself in the middle of this quarrel. Why does he want to fire you, anyway?"

"There's nothing wrong with my work." Hannah's voice was tight.

"That doesn't answer the question I asked. What did he do, make a pass at you? And you slapped him, so now he wants his revenge?"

She didn't look at him. "He planned to marry me and spend Isobel's riches." Her voice was tight.

He tried, without much success, not to laugh. "And he dumped you when he got the bad news. No wonder you wouldn't sell the box for a paltry five hundred. What a disappointment that must have been, if you expected to buy him with Isobel's money. So now I suppose you're the one who wants revenge?"

"It's the only thing I live for." She sounded irritable.

He wondered if she knew how appealing the curve of her throat was, when she arched her neck to thrust out a defiant chin.

Cooper tented his fingers together and surveyed her while he thought. "You're asking a lot, you know. This masquerade is quite a step up from my offer of cold cash for the box. You could keep me dancing attendance on you for months before you find another position."

"As if I'd want to." A note of impatience crept into her voice. "But if that's what's worrying you, you could solve the problem with a snap of the fingers. You must know everyone in this city who has influence and power. If you were to recommend me—"

"You seriously believe that those powerful and influential people are going to take my recommendation seriously even though they think you're sleeping with me?"

Hannah shook her head. "There's no reason for them to believe that. Just because we'll be going to a few events together doesn't mean—"

"On the contrary. There's a great reason for them to believe it." He leaned back into the depths of the couch. Now that his mind was made up, he was very much at his ease. The only thing that remained was to see how she would react to his terms—and he was looking forward to that. "I'll do it, Hannah. On one condition."

She sounded wary. "What's that?"

"That you move in here. Into this condo." He watched her eyes dilate with shock, and he felt a little tremor of elation run through him.

Then he added, just because he liked the sound of it, "That you live with me."

CHAPTER FOUR

HANNAH was on her feet before she even knew she'd moved. She stared down at Cooper, who was sprawled across the couch. He looked as relaxed as a rag doll, except for the alertness in his quicksilver eyes. If it hadn't been for that, she might have doubted that he'd really said what she thought she'd heard.

Move in here. Live with me, he had said.

One thing was sure: the sooner that notion was shot down, the better. "That's absolutely impossible."

In an easy gesture, Cooper held out both hands, palms up. "You know how negotiation works, Hannah. You put a proposition on the table, and I made a counteroffer. Now we talk."

"But there's nothing to talk about! What you've suggested isn't even—"

"Then you're welcome to call off the whole discussion."

But she couldn't simply walk away, and it was apparent to her that Cooper knew it just as well as she did. There was a gleam of satisfaction in his eyes, as if he thought he'd backed her into an inescapable corner.

He was wrong about that, of course; Hannah still had a few options, and even if she didn't like them much herself, there was no need for him to know that. "It would serve you right if I went straight out to the courtyard, started a bonfire and barbecued the Lovers' Box!"

"As Ken Stephens so painfully reminded me today, it's yours. You can do whatever you like with it."

But she noted that he'd hesitated for the barest fraction of a second before he'd said it. He wasn't as calm about the prospect as he would like her to think he was. "You're bluffing. You wouldn't stand by while I burned it."

"I'd much rather you didn't," he admitted. "But there are limits on what I'm willing to pay, and I warned you about that this afternoon, long before you came up with this crazy scheme."

"You're bluffing," she repeated.

"If I am—which I'm not conceding—then so are you, Hannah. You wouldn't destroy that box because it would leave you with no bargaining power over me at all, and you'd still have the problem with your boss." He sat up enough to reach for a handful of popcorn. "Where is the box now, by the way?"

The question was so casual that despite herself Hannah started to laugh. "You're very smooth, you know that?"

"I only meant that I hoped you didn't leave it in the apartment, where the movers might take it away as they're packing up Isobel's furniture."

"Of course that's all you meant," she mocked. "Just so we're clear about this, it will do you no good to search the condo because the box isn't there. It's put away very safely where only I can get it—in a bank vault, actually. And I won't tell you which bank."

"Good."

She was puzzled. "You're pleased?"

"Of course. All the banks are closed. That means you can't get to it tonight to burn it—so you might as well cool off and consider my offer."

She put her hands on her hips. "So we're back to that nonsense." Under the weight of her hand, something in the pocket of her suit jacket scratched her hip, even through the heavy fabric. It wasn't sharp, exactly, just annoying.

"It's not nonsense. Moving in with me makes perfect sense. Living together would be the easiest and fastest way to convince people we're a couple—and you did assure me that's what you want your boss to think."

"I want to convince him you're serious about me. I don't want him to get the idea that I've gone totally insane."

"There's nothing insane about it. Anyway, Hannah, I invited you to live with me, not sleep with me."

She was wary. "You're not trying to blackmail me into bed?"

Cooper threw back his head and started to laugh.

Hannah didn't quite know whether to be offended because he found the idea so hilarious or intrigued because, when he was relaxed and amused, he was a man she'd never seen before.

When he recovered himself, Cooper shook his head. "I've never descended to blackmail where a woman was concerned, and I have no intention of starting anytime soon. However, as long as we're on the subject of beds—"

Hannah gritted her teeth and swore to herself that she would not rise to the bait.

"It's particularly reasonable that you'd move in with me right now, considering that you no longer even have a bed down in Isobel's place."

Hannah was startled. "How did you know that? Oh, you must have run into the workmen in the elevator, too."

Was it her imagination, or did he hesitate for just an instant before he answered? "Kitty Stephens told me."

"So that's where she disappeared to when she was supposed to be supervising," Hannah mused. "She came up here. Lucky guy—to have won Kitty's heart without even taking her to lunch. She must not have stayed long, though.''

''No,'' Cooper said almost grimly. ''She didn't.''

Hannah gave a soundless whistle. ''Didn't let her past the door, hmm? I guess I should be flattered that you even allowed me to come in. As far as moving, though, you're far from my only option. I have friends. I could probably even stay with Mrs. Patterson for a while.''

''In her teeny little apartment—I think that's what you called it. You'd probably have to sleep in Brutus's bed.''

''Better Brutus's bed than yours,'' Hannah muttered.

He smiled. ''Since you haven't experienced either, how would you know which you prefer? In any case, moving in here may not be your only option but it's the best and most sensible one. If, that is, you really want this act to be convincing.''

As a matter of fact, Hannah could think of a dozen good reasons why a woman *wouldn't* actually move in with a man—even one she adored and planned to marry, and even if she found herself temporarily homeless. But all of those scenarios assumed a real relationship which was no one else's business—not one which was being manufactured purely for public view.

If Hannah had her own home, no one would be likely to question her staying there rather than rushing to move in with Cooper. But if, when she was forced from Isobel's condo, she turned to a friend instead of the supposed love of her life...or moved into a hotel...or grabbed the first furnished apartment she could find...

It would look odd, she admitted—and in this case, image was everything. Cooper, man of the world that he was, had put his finger straight on the problem that Hannah should have anticipated. He was right; this charade would be a lot more convincing if they were sharing a roof.

Move in here. Live with me.

She eyed him warily. She should find it reassuring, she told herself, that he'd laughed at the very idea of taking her into his bed. That reaction should have left no doubt in her mind that she'd be every bit as safe here as if she signed herself into a convent.

Hannah stuck her hands in her pockets while she thought about it. The sharp object that had poked her earlier, she realized, was only the corner of the foil packet containing her unused tea bag; she must have unthinkingly dropped it in her pocket instead of putting it back in the canister when she couldn't find a cup.

Now it was a concrete sign of how very few options she had left.

"Why would you want me around all the time?" she asked with honest curiosity. "You don't like me, you consider me a nuisance... What could possibly be the advantage of having me underfoot?"

"I wouldn't exactly call having you here an advantage—but if you don't have to worry about finding a place to live, you can spend all your time looking for a job instead."

"And be out of your hair that much faster."

Cooper admitted, "I'm not big on open-ended commitments."

"I'd noticed. Of course, now that I think of it, there's also the fact that if I'm right here, I can protect you from people like Kitty Stephens."

He snorted. "The day I need protection from a fluffy baby doll like that one—"

"Don't underestimate her," Hannah warned. "Daddy's girl is in the habit of getting whatever she wants. In fact, if I move in here, she's apt to start visiting me as an excuse to see you..." She frowned thoughtfully. "Oh, now I think

I've got it. Putting on a show of being serious about me means that you'll have to stop dating other women.''

Cooper's eyebrows climbed. ''Be careful what you say, Hannah, or you may make me think twice about agreeing to this farce.''

''I'm sure you must already have thought of that little side effect.'' Hannah's voice was airy. ''It was probably the first disadvantage that crossed your mind—not only how you'd handle it, but how all the women would. In fact, I'm betting that's why you suggested I move in.''

''And I'm sure you're planning to share your logic with me.''

''You've figured out that if I was living here, you could still see every last one of them and you wouldn't even have to be discreet about it. You could invite any or all of them to drop in, just by pretending they're really my friends instead.''

Cooper said dryly, ''I'm glad to see you're getting into the spirit of things.''

''But if I was living somewhere else, you wouldn't be able to entertain your female visitors without blowing the whole charade. If you did keep seeing the hordes of women, somebody would be bound to notice that your life hadn't changed a bit.''

''And they'd think it meant that I *wasn't* head over heels in love with you?'' he mused. ''Imagine that.''

''Whereas, with me living here, it's all easy. *Our* feminine friends arrive, I disappear, you have fun, everybody's happy. Well, now that we're clear about everything…'' Hannah pulled the tea bag out of her pocket and waved it at him. ''The movers had already packed up all of Isobel's china by the time I got home. Would you mind if I heated some water?''

"As long as you promise not to throw it at me," Cooper said, "make yourself at home."

The ironic twist in his voice made Hannah pause in midstep. "Thanks," she said. "I guess I will."

Even though she tried to convince him that she didn't need help, Cooper went downstairs with Hannah to retrieve her belongings. "It's the least any gentleman should do when a lady moves in with him," he insisted, and Hannah bit her tongue rather than argue about it, because from the gleam in his eyes, she knew he expected her to.

The movers had gone, and instead of the muffled silence Hannah had come to expect each time she stepped into Isobel's condo, every sound produced an empty echo.

With the furniture gone, the rooms looked tired, almost dreary. Deep dents in the carpet were the only remaining evidence of Isobel's furniture, and dirty streaks showed where the movers had dragged the pieces around.

Cooper stopped just inside the living room. "I suppose I'd better warn my mother right away that this place is going to need some serious work."

Hannah frowned. "What's she got to do with it?"

"Who do you think owns the condo now?"

"Not your mother, surely. Ken Stephens said something about a trust."

"He meant the family foundation."

"Damn," Hannah said. "I could have swapped the Lovers' Box for the condo, even up."

"Don't bet on it. The foundation is Mother's baby, not mine. I just sit on the board for appearance's sake." He looked around with distaste. "And speaking of appearances, the love nest is a lot more worn down than the last time I saw it."

Hannah paused in midstep. "You mean you've been here before?"

"You surely don't think Isobel would have given up the home court advantage while we were negotiating over the Lovers' Box."

"She insisted you come here to talk about it?" Hannah could almost picture the scene. "And I'll bet she made you sit on one of those dainty little chairs that were about as strong as toothpicks, and she poured tea and gave you watercress sandwiches—"

"Not at all. The old lady was much more subtle than you give her credit for being, Hannah. She made sure I had the best upholstered chair in town, because such a big strong man as me couldn't possibly be comfortable in anything less. Then she served me a stiff Scotch and water— and though there was a catch in her voice, she didn't quite wipe away a tear as she recalled how the last drink poured from that bottle had been the final one she ever fixed for my grandfather."

Hannah was fascinated. "You know, I've reconsidered. I wouldn't blame you if you *had* dropped arsenic in her glass."

"It was pretty good Scotch, too," Cooper mused. "All that extra aging hadn't hurt it a bit. If, of course, she was telling the truth in the first place."

"You actually *drank* it?"

He looked surprised. "Of course I did. It's not as if Scotch sours if it sits around too long. Besides, if I hadn't, she'd have known her manipulation was getting to me and she'd have kept right on playing the game. I wonder if the rest of the bottle is still here. If my grandfather really did pay for it in the first place—"

"Feel free to look. I'm going to pack up my clothes."

If the movers had stacked her belongings with a forklift,

they couldn't have made more of a mess. Hannah sighed and started dumping things into her suitcases at random; everything would have to be pressed before she could wear it anyway.

When she returned to the living room with her overnight bag, Cooper was standing across the room with his back to her, hands braced against the low mantel. She studied him for a moment and frowned. "Are you all right?"

He turned. "Sure. Why?"

"You looked as if you were having a heart attack or something." As she set the suitcase down at his feet, Hannah caught a glimpse of what he'd been looking at, a photograph which had been left lying on the mantel. "I suppose that's a picture of your grandfather."

Cooper nodded. "That's Irving, in his prime."

"*Irving?* That was really his name? That photo used to be in a silver frame on Isobel's dressing table. At least the movers left the picture instead of throwing it away. If you want it—"

"It would only remind me of where I found it." He reached for the overnight bag. "Is this all?"

"There are two more suitcases in the back bedroom. Oh, and that box." She picked up the carton of Jacob Jones's papers that she had so painstakingly carried home from the office.

"That's it? This is all you own?"

"No, but it's everything I brought with me when I moved in. The rest is in a storage shed out in the suburbs. None of it seemed to fit with Isobel's style." She balanced the box atop the overnight case while Cooper went after the rest of her luggage.

She'd never inspected the photograph on Isobel's dressing table; on occasion, when she'd been sent to bring Isobel a lipstick or a perfume spritz, she'd admired the elaborate silver frame but hadn't paid much attention to the face inside. Now she looked more carefully at the man who had been... what? The love of Isobel's life, or nothing more than a convenient meal ticket?

She could see bits of Cooper in him, though the older man had never been as tall or as good-looking as his grandson. The eyes were the same, and the strong lines of the jaw. But there the resemblance ended. Or was it only her imagination, fed by knowledge of his lifestyle, which made her think there was a slyness in Irving's face which had no counterpart in Cooper's? To say nothing of the thinning gray hair or the slightly pudgy waistline...

She slid the photo into the zipper pocket on the front of her overnight bag. She wasn't sure why, though it made sense not to simply leave it on the mantel to be tossed away by the cleaning crew which would no doubt take over by tomorrow.

One thing she had to admit about Cooper, she conceded; he was straightforward. What he wanted, he went after—without pretense, without manipulation...

"Well, without *much*," she muttered.

"Without much what?" he asked.

She hadn't heard him come back, carrying her suitcases with ease. "Delay," Hannah said quickly. "It must be getting awfully late."

"Not especially, but you've had a long day. Going from heiress to homeless in the space of a few hours—"

She was annoyed. "Are we back to this again? I thought you'd got the message by now that I never expected to get rich from Isobel's estate."

"I suppose next you'll be telling me that what's-his-name—the boss—got the idea entirely on his own that you were going to inherit a fortune."

"I wouldn't waste my time."

"That's what I thought," Cooper murmured.

In the penthouse, he showed her down a long hall in the opposite direction from the den where they'd talked earlier, to a large and very feminine guest room with an attached bath.

"You probably have everything you need," Cooper said. "But if not, check the linen closet in the bathroom. It should be pretty well stocked."

Hannah noted the lacy bedspread, ruffled pillows, silky drapes, and elegant dressing table. "I'm not saying I'm surprised at the idea of you having a lot of female overnight guests," she said. "But don't they get suspicious when they open the linen closet and see a whole case of new toothbrushes?"

"Surely you don't think that the sort of female overnight guest you're referring to ever sees this room."

Hannah grinned. "I deserved that—complete with the haughty tone." She set the box of papers on the edge of the dressing table.

Cooper was lounging against the door. "My bedroom is farther down, at the end of the hall."

"Thanks for the warning. I'll do my best to stay out of the vicinity."

"It wasn't a warning," Cooper assured her. "But it occurred to me just now that when you change your mind about sleeping with me, it would be a shame if you didn't know where to start looking."

Hannah could feel steam rising in her blood. "What happened to the saintly declaration that you weren't interested in one-night stands or long-term affairs?"

"I'm not. But I didn't say anything about the sort of thing that falls in between."

So much, Hannah thought, for the fleeting and naive belief that he wasn't the manipulative sort!

Cooper pushed himself away from the door. "And before you remind me that I said I wouldn't blackmail you into bed..." He smiled, and his eyes sparkled. "I didn't promise not to try persuasion." With the gentle touch of a finger under her chin, he tipped her face up to his.

The brush of his lips against hers was brief and feather-light, and before Hannah could react he was gone.

Suggesting that she move in with him, Cooper thought as he checked the locks and turned off the lights, had been a stroke of sheer genius.

Every single reason he'd given Hannah was absolutely factual. And so were the ones he hadn't mentioned.

Her scheme hadn't been bad, but the problem with it was that she hadn't gone nearly far enough to be convincing. With the little twist he'd added, the whole city would know by the end of the week—or, far more important, think they knew—that the two of them were lovers. She'd be able to stop watching her back at Stephens & Webster and get busy looking for a job, and just as soon as she found one, they'd be finished with this scheme.

If she'd been telling the truth about having no intention of engaging in an affair, then the forced intimacy of living together, spiced with the occasional stolen kiss and the like, would make her even more determined to get away from Stephens & Webster—and Cooper, of course—in a hurry.

And if she hadn't been telling the truth about her reluctance to sleep with him...well, he thought he'd laid the groundwork rather nicely for that, too. So long as she clearly understood the rules and didn't deceive herself into thinking that she could play him the way Isobel had maneuvered his grandfather, it wouldn't hurt Cooper's feelings a bit to dally with Hannah Lowe.

As a result, she'd either be out of his hair at the speed of light and he could get on with his life, or he'd have an entertaining few weeks first.

Whichever way it turned out, Cooper thought, he would end up the winner. If she really was as prim and straitlaced as she pretended to be, he'd soon cease to find that attitude diverting and his fascination with Hannah would wither and die.

If, instead, she intended to inveigle him into an affair, he'd no doubt allow her to succeed—but they'd be dealing with seduction on his terms, not hers. And with no mystery or distance left to increase the intrigue, his enchantment with Hannah would quickly wear itself out.

In either case, he'd have succeeded in wiping Hannah Lowe out of his mind once and for all.

And no matter which it turned out to be, before long he'd have the Lovers' Box safely back where it belonged, too. Whether he got it fair and square or sweet-talked her out of it in the midst of making love to her didn't much matter to Cooper, as long as he got what he wanted.

After all, he wasn't the one who'd been unreasonable in the first place.

He strolled down the hall to his bedroom, past the guest room he'd given Hannah. The masonry walls, part of the original old hotel, were too thick to allow any sound to pass, but he knew she was in there—unpacking, moving around to settle her things and herself. Or maybe she was already curled up under the quilted comforter—a small, warm, inviting bundle.

There were all sorts of benefits to this plan of his. Cooper could hardly wait for the rewards to start appearing.

Since he'd missed his regular evening walk the night before because of Hannah's other activities, Brutus was in no mood to cut short his early-morning exercise. Neither bribes nor orders made any impression on the dog at all, and by the time he'd sniffed every pole, tree, fireplug, and clump of grass along his regular route, Hannah was ready to scream.

At Stephens & Webster, being late for work was a risky career move, no matter what the reason. But being late after the scene she'd had with Brenton last night would be suicidal. And she was stuck not only with walking to work, but with carrying the carton of Jacob Jones's papers she'd brought home last night. Whatever had made her think *that* was a good idea?

As she finished the world's fastest shower, she reflected glumly that on a morning like this, she should probably be glad she'd remembered the box at all.

She had no time to enjoy the luxury of her new quarters, or to look around at the rest of Cooper's penthouse. But one thing was sure, she told herself as she hastily pinned her hair into a French twist: if this was merely the guest quarters, the rest of the place must be well worth the price of a ticket if he ever opened it up for tours again.

She scooped up the box of papers and hurried toward the front entrance. At a turn in the hall she almost bumped into a gray-haired gentleman in a severe black suit, and she gave a little shriek.

He, on the other hand, seemed completely unperturbed. "Good morning, Ms. Lowe. I am Abbott, the butler. Mr. Winston is waiting for you in the breakfast room. I believe you already know where the den is? Go on just past it and turn left." He bowed slightly and proceeded down the hall.

Hannah stared after him for a moment. "And a very well-informed butler, too," she muttered. She wasn't surprised that he knew her name. But how did he know which areas of the house she'd already been in? Or did Cooper habitually take his feminine companions to his den?

"Not likely," she sniffed, and found her way to the breakfast room.

Cooper set aside the morning paper and half rose. "You look as if you've seen a ghost."

"I suppose I do. I ran into the butler—and for just an instant I thought it was your grandfather."

"Oh, no," Cooper said easily. "If Irving was going to haunt anyone, it would have been Isobel. Besides, though there is a superficial resemblance, Abbott is by far more aristocratic than my grandfather was. If you'd known them both, you couldn't possibly mistake one for the other." He gestured to a chair. "Mrs. Abbott has made waffles for breakfast, unless you'd prefer something else."

"You have a housekeeper, too?" Hannah didn't sit down. "I don't have time to eat anything. I'm due at work in half an hour and it takes twenty minutes to walk the distance." She hesitated. "Maybe tonight we can figure out a plan of action—exactly how we're going to start convincing the world."

Cooper raised his voice. "Mrs. Abbott, is there a waffle ready?"

Hannah said, "But I—"

"I'll take you to the office."

Hannah sat down. "That should start the process off nicely," she conceded. "Getting out of your car in front of the main door while everyone's streaming into work—"

"As for convincing the world, I think it would be best to say as little as possible to anyone about how and when this affair of ours started." He broke off as a woman in a print dress and spotless white apron brought in a steaming waffle. "Thank you, Mrs. Abbott."

Hannah watched as the housekeeper retreated. "She

heard every word you said, and she didn't even blink. How long have the Abbotts been here?''

"Longer than I have. They worked for my grandparents.''

"I see. In that case she's had a chance to get used to this sort of thing.''

He frowned. "I don't think that my grandfather ever brought Isobel here.''

"I wasn't talking about your grandfather's affairs,'' Hannah said sweetly. "All right—where were we? Oh, yes, you were saying we should let people believe whatever they like about how long this has been going on.''

"We certainly don't want your boss to figure out that it coincidentally began right after that fight you had with him.''

"It wasn't a fight,'' she corrected. "And wouldn't it be better to say straight-out that we've been dating since right after the sale of your restaurant chain?''

"No, because too many people would know it isn't accurate. If we just say that we've been seeing each other casually for quite a while—the more vague the time frame, the better—nobody can argue.''

"Besides, that tale has the benefit of being true,'' Hannah mused. "It's been close to six weeks since Brutus first threatened to bite you—that's quite a while. And ever since then we've been running into each other at every turn—that's seeing each other casually.''

"We were being very discreet about our attraction to each other—''

Hannah laughed. "So discreet even we didn't know it!''

"Now that we've both realized how serious we are, however, we're coming out in the open with it.'' Cooper glanced at his watch. "Starting fifteen minutes from now, directly in front of Stephens & Webster.''

Precisely four minutes before Hannah was due at her desk, Cooper's black Ferrari pulled up in the fire lane in front of the law firm's office building. Hannah slid out and waved casually at one of the receptionists, who stopped dead in the middle of the sidewalk, eyes wide.

Hannah was trying to maneuver the carton of papers from the infinitesimal back seat when Cooper came around the car and said, "Let me get that, darling."

He was good, Hannah admitted. He had captured just the right careless tone—not at all as if it was the first time he'd ever said the word. *But of course it isn't really the first time,* she reminded herself. *It's just that he's never said it to me before. I'm the only thing that's changed.* "I can lift a box of papers, Cooper."

He gave her an affectionate pat on the bottom.

Hannah straightened up so fast she almost knocked herself out on the edge of the car door. "What in the—"

"You deserve a spanking for not letting me help. Besides, since I'm not going to see you till lunchtime, I need something to tide me over."

He put a casual arm around her shoulders and drew her close. Instinctively, Hannah stiffened and turned her face away, only to see Brenton Bannister standing just a few feet away, looking as dumbfounded as the receptionist had.

Obviously, she thought, Cooper had twenty-twenty peripheral vision, to have spotted her boss at that angle. She relaxed into his arms and smiled up at him, raising one hand to brush her fingertips along his jaw. "Sorry, sweetheart. I just—well, I've gotten used to being discreet where you're concerned."

She saw something that might have been amusement flicker in his eyes. "We'd better break that attitude down before it becomes a habit," he murmured, and before

Hannah could brace herself, he was kissing her as if they were alone in the universe.

Her knees were the first thing to go, but the rest of her wasn't far behind, and by the time Cooper finished, Hannah's entire body felt like a toasted marshmallow—melted mush on the inside, barely held together by a pleasantly singed exterior.

And he'd done it, she thought fuzzily, without moving a hand beyond her shoulders. He'd done nothing off-color, nothing that even the most prudish of onlookers could have called distasteful—and yet anyone who had gotten a glimpse of that display couldn't possibly doubt that they were lovers.

She had to make a special effort to open her eyes, and it took a moment for her to focus well enough to see that Brenton Bannister was no longer on the sidewalk.

"You might not be used to public displays of affection," Cooper said a little gruffly, "but you're good at them."

"It's apparently like dancing." Hannah was having trouble getting her breath. "It only takes one expert to guide the action. Thanks."

This time there was no doubt about the amusement in his eyes. "It was entirely my pleasure, Hannah."

"It's a good thing you saw Brenton coming, because I missed him at first."

"Your boss?" Cooper didn't sound interested. "Was he there?"

Hannah felt like kicking him. If he honestly hadn't seen Brenton...but of course he had; he was just pulling her chain. "You don't think I threw myself into that scene just for the practice, do you?"

He grinned. "My dear, I have no idea what you're capable of doing. But I must say I'm looking forward to finding out."

CHAPTER FIVE

HANNAH was still trying to overcome the all-gone feeling left over from Cooper's kiss when she reached her cubicle office. But instead of sanctuary and a chance to catch her breath, she found Brenton sitting at her desk, feet propped up on the corner of the shiny surface and fingers tented.

He'd taken the position deliberately, she was sure, knowing that confiscating her chair would tend to make her feel out of place in her own office, as if she'd been summoned for discipline. And if she asked him to move, he'd simply point out that he'd only been making himself comfortable while he waited for her.

Unwilling to stand still for that treatment, Hannah walked around the desk and seated herself on the corner his feet weren't occupying.

She waited patiently until he twisted around to study her. It appeared, she thought, as if he didn't much like having to look up at her. But any hope that he might simply take the hint and leave quickly evaporated.

His voice was almost a growl. "No wonder you turned down my invitation to dinner last night."

Hannah was startled. That kind of accusation was the last thing she'd have expected. Was the man delusional? Did he really believe that she had refused him, rather than him standing her up? Or was he setting some kind of a trap for her?

She bit her tongue and waited.

"It's awfully funny I haven't got a hint of anything

82

about this before. You've obviously been trying to keep Cooper Winston under wraps.''

Hannah shrugged. ''Not particularly, but I always figured my love life was my own business, not the firm's.''

''So you were just being discreet yesterday when you told me Winston would never bring his business to Stephens & Webster. Well, I'd say it's pretty strange that you chose this particular day to suddenly decide to be indiscreet for a change.''

''Why is it strange? After last night—''

Brenton sat up, his feet hitting the floor with a thump. ''Exactly. After last night—''

Hannah felt as if she were walking through a mine field. ''I was afraid you'd take it personally when I turned down your invitation,'' she said with only a hint of irony. ''And since I didn't want you to think I'd refused because I didn't like you—'' *Even though it's true.* ''—I talked it over with Cooper last night, and—''

''And decided to put on a show.''

That, Hannah thought, was uncomfortably close to the truth. ''We decided it was a little silly to keep hiding our attraction for each other, because we might give others the wrong impression about our availability. We've been together long enough now that we both know we're serious, so why try to keep it secret any longer?''

Brenton pounced. ''You said a couple of minutes ago that you *weren't* trying to keep it secret.''

''I just meant we weren't taking out ads to announce it. But there's a big difference between acting casual and being secretive—we haven't exactly been sneaking around in trench coats and dark glasses so no one would see us together.''

Brenton grunted, but he didn't pursue the subject.

Hannah had to stifle the urge to sigh in relief; this wasn't over yet.

"Why didn't you tell me yesterday that Winston figured in Isobel's will, too?"

"I didn't think you'd be particularly interested," Hannah said dryly. "How did you happen to hear that, anyway?"

Brenton ignored the question. "So did he get it all? Is that why you're so interested in him all of a sudden?"

"It isn't sudden. I've been seeing him since right after our client bought his restaurants." It wasn't quite a lie, Hannah told herself. It had been just a few days after the deal was signed that she and Brutus had started their walks, and on their very first excursion the pug had threatened to bite Cooper... "Anyway, I told you there was nothing to get. Isobel's cupboards were truly bare."

She wondered, idly, where Brenton was getting his information. Not from Ken Stephens, surely—or it would have been more complete and accurate. But who did that leave? Someone who had seen them both going into Ken's office yesterday?

Or Kitty? Hannah wouldn't be surprised if—with one avenue to riches suddenly closed to him—Brenton had moved quickly to capitalize on another.

She lifted her briefcase to the desk blotter, snapped it open, and began taking out folders. "Anyway, since I'm not inheriting Isobel's fictional millions, I have a living to earn. So if you don't mind—"

"Odd," Brenton murmured. "I'd have thought Winston would be more generous than that with his doxies."

Hannah gritted her teeth. *It's only a word,* she reminded herself. And the very fact he had used it indicated that her plan had been more successful than she'd dared to hope.

So much for Cooper's notion that they would have to live under the same roof in order to be convincing!

Of course, she reminded herself, Cooper obviously had a few of his own reasons for that suggestion, and persuading Brenton hadn't been at the top of his personal list. Her boss had simply provided him with a handy excuse to keep Hannah close at hand. And going on the evidence of last night, the real reason he wanted her that close was to seduce her.

Persuasion, indeed! It would serve Cooper right, she decided, if she moved out just as fast as she'd moved in— before anyone even knew that she'd taken up residence in the penthouse.

She should be relieved at the very idea that she could escape, she thought. So why was she feeling just a little let down instead?

"Too bad for you if the facts sting," Brenton said briskly. "I believe in telling it like it is. What I actually came in for was the box of papers you took home last night. I'm ready to start reviewing the Jones case and I want to start with those."

The box, Hannah realized, that was still riding around the city in the back of Cooper's Ferrari, forgotten in the aftermath of their award-winning performance in front of the building.

Now what? she asked herself. It wasn't going to sit well with Brenton if she had to admit she'd casually left a client's property in a car. And not just any car, but one belonging to a man who had good reason to want to discredit Stephens & Webster… No. She couldn't tell Brenton that. She might as well go hang herself in the ladies' room as admit to such an egregious violation of the firm's rules about safeguarding the property of clients.

But—since she didn't know how much of that scene in

front of the building that Brenton had witnessed this morning—she could hardly tell him anything but the truth, either. If there was any chance at all that he had overheard their discussion of who was going to lift the box out of the car...

And he must have been listening, Hannah realized. There was no reason to single out that particular box—unless he expected that she couldn't produce it anytime soon.

The trouble was, he was right.

Brenton picked up the phone and held it out to her. "Let me make it easy for you," he said. "All you have to do is call Winston and tell him to bring the box straight back."

If only it were that easy, Hannah thought. She could hardly call Cooper when she didn't have a hint of where he'd been going after he dropped her off. She could probably explain the fact that she didn't know the details of his schedule for the day; Cooper didn't know about all of her appointments, either. But to have to admit that she didn't have the number of his cell phone—

How serious could a man be if he hadn't even given the special woman in his life his private phone number?

She was reasonably sure that Cooper had intended that kiss to blow away her inhibitions. She wasn't so certain that he'd planned to short-circuit her brain, as well, but that seemed to be what had happened. How had she gotten herself into this mess? And how was she going to get out?

"He hates being interrupted at work," she said. "I'll have it back by lunchtime." It was a pretty lame explanation, but it was the best she could do.

"So you did leave it in his car," Brenton mused.

Damn, Hannah thought. He hadn't known for certain, till she'd helpfully told him.

"Those were the most recent of Jones's papers, weren't they?"

Hannah, who had not yet opened that particular box, didn't have a clue. But it had been a very direct question, and there wasn't an easy way to avoid answering, so she'd just have to take her chances. The box hadn't been as ragged as some of the others, she recalled. "I believe so, yes."

"But obviously you don't know for certain." Brenton's eyes were hooded. "I've noticed lately that you have a problem with inattention to detail, Hannah. Perhaps I should remind you that your employee review is coming up."

"Not for another four months—when I've been here a full year." *And with any luck, I'll be gone long before then.*

Brenton smiled. "I've decided to do them early. That way I can get the paperwork done and put my staff's minds at ease about the quality of their work. And, of course, if we discover problems to be corrected, we can start right away to straighten out the difficulties. I thought I'd begin with you."

She said, wryly, "That's very thoughtful of you."

"Of course, I could be prepared to overlook a few bits of carelessness if the rest of your job performance measured up to my standards."

In other words, Hannah thought, he was prepared to commit a little studied inattention to detail himself, in the name of getting what he wanted. She said, steadily, "And just what do you have in mind, Brenton?"

Stopping at the reception desk to ask for directions had been a waste of time, Cooper decided. The verbal road map the receptionist had given him was worse than useless; it was almost impossible to find one's way to a specific cubicle among the long rows of sound-deadening panels which filled an entire floor of Stephens & Webster's offices.

Nothing could be more unlike the elegance of the senior partners' offices upstairs. No wonder every meeting which had taken place here concerning the sale of the restaurant chain had been held in a conference room on the topmost floor, rather than in this rat's nest.

He shifted the weight of Hannah's box of papers and passed three more empty cubicles, hoping that she hadn't stepped out to the copy machine or the mail room. If she had, he might never discover which dead end in this maze belonged to Hannah. What was a visitor supposed to do, he wondered—stand still and scream a name till someone answered?

He turned a corner and glanced into another cubicle, and a faint hint of musky perfume, combined with the sight of an elegantly-arched neck under upswept chestnut-colored hair, told him he'd reached his destination. With her back to the cubicle's entrance, Hannah was concentrating on the screen of a laptop computer set up on the bookshelf behind her desk.

Cooper set the box down on her desk and leaned over to kiss the enticing spot where her hairline dipped toward the collar of her jacket. At the first touch, she sat up straight, grabbing for the computer's controls, and the back of her head smacked hard into his nose. "Ouch," Cooper protested. "Is that any way to treat the man you adore?"

Hannah wheeled her chair around and looked up, wide-eyed. "Sorry. I didn't hear you at first, and I thought it might be Brenton spying on me, even though he's supposed to be in conference." She clicked a couple of buttons, and the screen, which had abruptly gone dark, began to glow again.

"What are you doing? Updating your résumé?"

"No, that's done. I was looking up a headhunter firm on the Internet."

With his thumb and index finger, Cooper gently wiggled the end of his nose. "I guess there's no serious damage done."

"Not to you, maybe. You scared me half to death."

"Is that the thanks I get for returning your box of papers? Not that I'm expecting lots of credit, because I wouldn't even have remembered the thing was there if it hadn't been for the way it made the car smell."

"Sorry. I think our client stored his records in a root cellar."

"Don't insult root cellars. They smell much nicer than that box does. Let's try this again." With the nape of her neck out of reach, he settled for the soft triangle below her ear. "You do, too."

"I do what?"

"Smell much nicer than the box." His mouth lingered against the velvety skin. He could feel the flutter of her pulse against his lips; she wasn't quite as calm as she'd like him to think. Her perfume was very subtle today, with only a hint of the same musky scent Isobel had worn mixed with something fresher and even more appealing. He wanted to bury his face in her neck and breathe slowly until he'd had time to sort out the aromas. But she was obviously growing restive, so he let her go and perched on the edge of the desk, giving the box a nudge. "I'd heard that the practice of law sometimes had an unpleasant stink, but I always thought it was a figure of speech. What is this stuff, anyway?"

"It's a tax case. I can't tell you any more, but I have

to go through every invoice and receipt for the last five years. Not that I think it will do Mr. Jones much good, because I'm convinced the evidence that would save his neck isn't there. Probably it never existed.''

''He's a crook?'' Cooper kept his tone casual.

She smiled a little. ''You didn't hear that from me.''

He picked up the top invoice and dropped it back into the box. ''Every single paper, hmm? No wonder you want a new job.''

''I'm working on it.'' She waved a hand at the computer.

''I'd think you'd grab at anything to escape this kind of dull chore.''

''Not every minute is this dull—researching the law relevant to a particular case is a lot more interesting, and that's mostly what I do. But associates at any law firm get the tedious detail work. Somebody has to do it. Besides, it's like a trial by fire.''

''What's it supposed to prove?''

''Persistence, for one thing.''

It sounded more like idiocy to him, Cooper thought. ''I was going to take you out to lunch, but if you're absorbed—''

''You certainly don't want to interrupt my job search, do you, Cooper?''

He thought it would be less than judicious to actually agree. ''We could order in. Or—since you didn't get your hot dog yesterday—I could go get a couple from the park around the corner.''

''Would you? That sounds really good. I'm glad you stopped by, though. Without a phone number, I didn't know how to let you know that I'm going to be here late tonight.''

''No, you're not.'' His tone was breezy.

She frowned at him. "Look, Cooper, if you think this agreement of ours gives you the right to dictate my schedule... Anyway, why would you want to? You've as good as admitted that you're every bit as anxious as I am for me to find a new job."

"Normally I wouldn't interfere, but tonight is different. We're giving a party."

Hannah looked exasperated. "What does that mean? You've invited all your women to drop in for dessert, so you only have to go over the new house rules once?"

"That would at least be an interesting party," Cooper mused. "Which this one emphatically won't be. I'd actually managed to forget about it till this morning, but it's been planned for weeks. That's why you have to appear."

"Because it would look suspicious if I didn't even try to arrange my schedule around it? I see. What kind of a party?"

"The worst. Cocktails and conversation—of a sort—with the bigwigs involved in the family charitable foundation."

"Including your mother, right?"

"She's looking forward to meeting you."

"I'll bet," Hannah said dryly.

"It's really her party, not mine. After she redecorated my penthouse, she likes to show it off. That's why I'd forgotten about it—along with the fact that these events are deadly dull."

"I could always invite Brenton to liven things up."

"I suppose you want me to impress him."

"Not exactly. I want you to imply that I've talked you into giving him some of your legal business. Otherwise, he assures me, he will confide in you that I had an affair with him and broke his heart when I decided to go after you instead."

She was perfectly cool about it, he observed. Almost calculating—with a momentary but uncanny resemblance to Isobel.

"And you don't want him to do that," Cooper mused.

"Of course not. As long as he thinks he's holding that over my head, he won't bother to make up something worse."

Her reasoning made sense. And he frankly didn't think she was capable of telling a whopper without turning beet-red; though she wasn't quite a redhead, her skin was so fair that she generally reacted like one.

And yet Cooper wondered idly whether he was giving Hannah too little credit. She surely hadn't gotten as far as she had in her profession without learning some self-control. Perhaps she wasn't entirely unlike Isobel after all. Isobel—who had had such perfect control of herself that she could blush at will...except, of course, that Isobel had probably never seen any reason to blush at all.

Was it possible that Hannah was reluctant to let Brenton share his story because it was actually true?

Even if that was so, probably not all of the tale was factual; Cooper doubted the bit about Hannah purposely going after him, because throwing a glass of red wine at a man wasn't the way a woman typically went about making herself attractive to him.

Though, on second thought, he had to admit the stunt had gotten his attention in a way no other feminine trick could have done....

Not that it mattered, whether it was true or not. Hannah Lowe's schemes—or lack of them—didn't affect him in the least. He'd enjoy her, get over her, and move on.

It was as dead simple as that.

The manager's office was already closed when Hannah reached Barron's Court that evening, but the doorman was in the lobby and she stopped to give him her key to Isobel's condo. "Now that I've moved out," she said, "I don't want to keep this. If I continue to have access, I could be held responsible if anything went wrong there." She pushed the elevator button.

The doorman looked at the brass key lying innocently in his palm. "But, Ms. Lowe," he said plaintively. "If you're not living here anymore—"

"Why am I going upstairs? It's a long story, Daniel."

"I've got all night."

Hannah glanced at the Art Deco clock on the lobby wall. "Well, I don't, if I'm going to be ready for the party. If you'd tell the mail room to deliver my letters to the penthouse for the present, I'd appreciate it."

The doorman looked at her with even more concern. "You're going to live in Mr. Winston's penthouse? In all the time I've been here, he's never had anybody to actually live with him."

And Daniel, Hannah thought, would certainly be the first to know. "In that case, I guess I should be honored to be the exception." She escaped into the elevator and leaned against the wall, eyes closed, trying to summon courage.

She was well and truly committed now. So much for her brief consideration of moving out; confiding in the doorman at Barron's Court was the equivalent of taking out a full-page ad in the local newspaper.

But even before she'd told Daniel about her move, it had been too late to change her mind. Obviously Cooper had already told his mother about the Lovers' Box and the agreement he and Hannah had made, and once he'd enlisted her help to spread the word there was no backing out. With the network Cooper's mother must have at her disposal, the grapevine would already be buzzing.

She's looking forward to meeting you, Cooper had said. Hannah didn't doubt it a bit.

If she survived the next few weeks, she thought, she could give up law entirely and go straight to the United Nations as a senior diplomat.

Inside the penthouse, controlled mayhem had broken out. In the dining room, the caterers were setting up; in the enormous living room a florist was putting the final touches on an arrangement of cut flowers atop a side table. From somewhere out of sight, the subdued roar of a vacuum cleaner formed a backdrop to the staccato give-and-take of questions and instructions.

A small woman in black was standing in the center of the foyer, her back to the door, when Hannah came in. The woman glanced at her watch, then stuck two fingers in her mouth and whistled. The sound sliced through and silenced every other noise in the penthouse, except for the bang of Hannah's leather briefcase as—taken aback by the unlady-like gesture—she dropped it on the stone floor.

"Fifteen-minute warning," the woman announced. She turned to face Hannah. "You're Hannah, of course. You're pushing it a bit close, too, aren't you?"

Obviously, Hannah thought as she saw the chilly look in the woman's fine-sculptured face, her guess had been correct. Cooper had indeed confided the whole story to his mother.

"I wouldn't want you to think I was neglecting my career," Hannah said coolly. "You might get the idea I was planning on this agreement with Cooper being more than a temporary situation."

The woman's eyebrows lifted. "You're not a bit like Isobel, are you? I'm Sarah Winston."

Hannah offered her hand. "Thank you. At least, I assume that was intended as a compliment?"

"Oh, yes. Isobel would have clothed that statement in sweet hypocrisy. I much prefer your honest sarcasm. Cooper warned me that I'd like you. I'm beginning to think he might be right."

Warned? What a curious way to put it, Hannah thought. She wondered if the warning had lain in Cooper's words or only in his mother's interpretation of them.

Before she could sort it out, Cooper appeared from the bedroom wing. "I see you two have met. Can I get you a drink before the guests start arriving, Mother?"

"No, let me do it," Sarah said briskly. "I need to check out the bar anyway to be certain it's set up properly. Something for you, Hannah?"

"Anything but red wine," Cooper said helpfully.

Sarah looked blank.

"Hannah doesn't drink it. She prefers to—"

Hannah stepped on his foot, hard. When he looked down at her in surprise, she cooed, "I'm so sorry, darling. I'm being terribly clumsy these days. You were saying…?"

"I was just going to tell Mother that when you showed me the damage which can result, in certain circumstances, from a single glass of red wine, you turned me into something of a temperance advocate, as well."

Sarah's bright gaze flickered between them. "I see," she murmured, and her sudden smile showed off unexpected dimples.

Disarmed, Hannah stared after her as the woman crossed the room and detoured to inspect the hors d'oeuvres buffet.

"Why didn't you want me to tell her about the wine?" Cooper asked.

Good question, Hannah thought. Why should it matter? If Sarah Winston knew all the other ins and outs of this bargain, why hesitate to share the joke about the glass of wine she'd thrown?

The doorbell rang, and she stepped back, at Cooper's urging, toward the big living room. The butler answered the door, and just as the first guests came toward them, Cooper slid a possessive arm around Hannah's shoulders.

The woman guest stopped as if she'd run into an invisible wall. The man who accompanied her, obviously less sensitive to nuances, came straight-on, hand outstretched. ''Well, well,'' he said. ''Who's this, Cooper, my boy?''

''This is Hannah,'' Cooper said. He was looking down at her, Hannah thought irritably, with very much the same expression in his eyes as if she'd been a tall, cold drink on a hot summer day. But it had the effect he'd apparently intended on his audience; the man laughed, while the woman looked reproachfully at Cooper and stared straight through Hannah.

As the couple moved toward the buffet table, the bell rang again, and soon they were awash in guests.

She was just starting to feel comfortable when she looked up to see Ken and Kitty Stephens in the doorway, with Brenton Bannister half a step behind. ''Oh, no,'' she said involuntarily and shot a look up at Cooper. ''What are they doing here? I can see Ken as a big contributor to your foundation, but Brenton Bannister, never.''

''Ken isn't a contributor, either—not yet. But just wait till my mother gets hold of him. I ran into him in the elevator at Stephens & Webster today as I was leaving after lunch. Since you'd said something about inviting Brenton, I thought I might as well expand the invitation to include Ken, too.''

''I was joking about inviting Brenton! Have you lost your mind?''

"It'll be easier to convince Brenton that we're a two-some if people he respects believe it."

"But we were sniping at each other in Ken Stephens's office just yesterday!"

Cooper drew himself up haughtily. "We were attempting to conceal our true feelings."

Despite herself, Hannah gave a little crow of laughter. "And doing it so well we managed to conceal them even from ourselves!" She sobered. "I still think it might have been a better idea to— Hello, sir. How nice to see you."

Ken took her hand with a conspiratorial wink. "You know, I wondered yesterday if there wasn't more to the story than was obvious, the sparks you two were striking off each other."

And no doubt if she pressed the subject, he'd stand there straight-faced and explain that was why he'd invited Cooper to lunch—so Kitty could quiz him about Hannah. *Good try, Ken,* Hannah thought wryly. Even Kitty looked as if she could choke on that one.

But right now, with Brenton watching them narrowly, was no time to let herself be distracted. "Brenton, I'm glad you could make it."

"I'm certain of that," Brenton said smoothly. "Tell me, who are you trying most to impress with your new status? Ken, or Kitty, or me?"

It was Cooper who answered. "Ken, of course—because Hannah's dual position with the law firm and the Winston family will make it much easier for my mother to ask him for money to help support the foundation's programs. Speaking of my mother, where has she gone?"

"Last time I saw her she was by the fireplace," Hannah said, and he turned to look for Sarah.

"You certainly fell into a tub of gravy, didn't you, Hannah?" Brenton murmured. "Play your cards right and you might not have to earn a living after all—at least not by practicing law. I'm sure you have other skills you could get Winston interested in.''

Hannah recognized the technique; long before professional athletes started using trash talk to annoy and upset their opponents, attorneys had mastered the skill. ''You consider making love to be work?'' she asked with mock concern. ''I expected you'd think it was more like a fringe benefit. Of course, I'm sure it all depends on *who*—''

She felt a hand on her shoulder, and beside her Sarah said, ''Someone said you were trying to get my attention, Cooper.''

''Here, Mother, I've got a prospect for you.''

Ken Stephens chuckled. ''A pigeon ripe for the plucking, he means.'' He reached out to the tiny woman in black, and his expression softened. ''Hello, Sarah. It's been a long, long time.''

Sarah studied his outstretched hand as if she'd never seen one before and had no idea what to do with it. Then she looked up into his face. ''On the contrary, Ken,'' she said in a voice so clear it rang out across the foyer. ''It hasn't been nearly long enough.''

She turned her back on him and walked away.

CHAPTER SIX

FASCINATED, Hannah watched as Ken Stephens's face slowly turned brick-red. He opened his mouth and then closed it again. It must be, she thought, the first time in years that the senior partner had been struck speechless. For him to stand there silent and absorb an insult like that one—

Sarah had gained Hannah's undiluted admiration.

Brenton gave a low whistle. "I wouldn't count on any sizable donations from that direction, Winston."

Obviously bewildered, Kitty stared at the gap in the crowd through which Sarah had disappeared. "Daddy, what did she mean? Do you even know her?"

Cooper raised one hand to the knot of his necktie and tugged at it.

Hannah said, under her breath, "I guess this means you also didn't tell your mother Ken was coming tonight? Maybe next time a little planning ahead might be wise." She stepped into the breach. "Kitty, Brenton—let me get you each a drink."

She linked her arm in Kitty's to draw the young woman away, and she heard Ken tell Cooper, "One thing about Sarah—she always lets you know where she stands."

"Whether you ask or not," Cooper muttered, and Ken gave a choked, awkward laugh.

Though the party had turned out to be far more exciting than Cooper had warned her it would, it threatened to be never-ending. Nobody seemed to want to leave, for fear of missing the next act in the drama.

Sarah obviously knew she was being closely watched, for she sparkled her way from group to group. Hannah noted, however, that she kept her distance from the corner where Ken stood.

Hannah thought irritably that he seemed to be impersonating a statue, for he didn't move except to take an occasional sip from his martini. And he seemed prepared to stand there all night. It wasn't until Kitty, with Brenton beside her, told him she was bored and was going on to a nightclub that Ken even appeared to realize where he was. Then he hastily finished his drink and made his farewells.

It took all of Hannah's self-control not to sigh in relief as the three departed. Just as she had expected, their exit seemed to be the crack in the dam; soon the rest of the guests formed a flood headed for the elevator, and within half an hour only Cooper and Hannah and Sarah were left in the penthouse.

The caterer's staff moved in like vultures to clear up the mess, and Cooper guided the two women back to his den.

Sarah said briskly, "I think I'll just run along. I'm sure the cleaning up will go just fine, and—"

Cooper closed the door and looked at her directly, his eyes narrowed. "I can understand the urge to cut Ken Stephens, Mother, but why in hell did you have to do it in public?"

Sarah raised her eyebrows. "Does the phrase *It's none of your business* strike a chord with you, Cooper?"

"I didn't say it was my business. But it's definitely the foundation's business."

"I don't see how," Sarah muttered. "If that man ever gave a dime to a good cause, I have yet to hear about it. The only thing he ever thought of was looking out for his own best interests. If you think you can put the touch on him for a big donation—"

Hannah braced herself for an explosion. But Cooper's voice was almost gentle. "You're the head of the family foundation, Mother. You can't go around insulting community leaders, no matter how much you dislike them or how good your reasons are. It makes you look like a vicious cat. If you don't believe me, ask Hannah."

Sarah looked abashed. "Was it that bad?"

Hannah wanted to kick Cooper; until that moment she'd have bet Sarah had forgotten all about her. "Not *bad* exactly," she said reluctantly. "I mean, if you don't want to associate with him, why should you have to? But if I hadn't known why you were so upset with him, I'd have been wondering who you were likely to take after next."

Cooper gave her an approving nod. Hannah wanted to stick her tongue out at him.

"And the fact is," he said, "that many of the people here tonight didn't know why you were so upset with Ken. They didn't know Irving or Isobel, much less know that Ken was Isobel's attorney—and they have no reason to care about any of it."

Sarah took a deep breath. "So what do you suggest I do about it? Apologize to Ken Stephens as publicly as I insulted him?"

"I'll leave that up to your judgment, Mother."

"I'm glad there's something you trust my judgment about," Sarah muttered. "Now, if the lecture's over, I think I'll go home."

When Cooper returned from walking his mother to her car, Hannah was just settling into the corner of the couch with a bowl of salsa and corn chips. "Thanks for dragging me into it," she said irritably. "Though why you thought your mother would take any notice of my opinion is beyond me."

Cooper dug a hand into the chips. "It worked."

"That's my point. It shouldn't have. If Sarah cut Ken dead just for being Isobel's attorney, she should want to string me up for being her cousin. Just the fact that I've got the Lovers' Box now..." She paused, frowning thoughtfully.

"You didn't have any choice about being related to Isobel, but Ken didn't have to be her attorney. He could have turned down her business." He dipped another chip in salsa and crunched it.

Hannah wasn't satisfied. "Do you really think that's all it was? It's not exactly easy to fire a client, you know— and surely your mother understands that ethically, once Isobel had hired him, Ken had to do the best he could for her."

"Doesn't mean she has to approve of his tactics, any more than I had to enjoy the fifteen-million-dollar ride you took me on."

"I didn't think you'd forgotten about that." Absent-mindedly Hannah stacked corn chips in an ungainly pile on her palm.

"And furthermore, I don't plan to let it slip my mind anytime soon." Cooper leaned over to inspect her palm, cupping his hand under hers so she couldn't pull away. "Interesting. Are there regular rules to this game, or do we make them up as we go along?" With the tip of his tongue, he captured the top chip and drew it into his mouth. "I've got it. You hold a chip between your lips and I'll nibble till it's gone, and then we'll change places."

Faintly, as if in the distance, Hannah heard the doorbell chime. Not quite sure whether to be relieved at the interruption or annoyed at having to face yet another social obligation, she said, "Are you expecting anyone?"

"No. Perhaps one of the guests came back to retrieve a

glove or something. Abbott will take care of it.'' He slid a little closer.

Hannah leaned back, away from him, and her hand closed convulsively on the pile of chips, crushing them almost to dust. "Probably Kitty," she said. "Or do you think she's capable of planning so far ahead?"

Cooper ignored the question. He captured her hand and slowly unfurled her fingers to reveal the remnants of her chips. His fingertips lingered along her palm, as he slowly picked up each fragment and transferred it to his mouth.

Hannah sat very still, willing herself to remain calm. It was apparent what Cooper was after, and it wasn't chips. He wanted to drive her crazy.

And, she was forced to admit, he was doing a pretty good job of it. She'd never realized before that the palm of her hand could be turned into an erotic playground...

Sheer stubbornness allowed her to hold out till the last infinitesimal chip was gone—but when she started to pull her hand away Cooper resisted and flicked his tongue against her lifeline. "Salt," he said. "You wouldn't deny it to a starving man, would you?"

"There's a whole bag of chips on the coffee table," she pointed out. "You can lick every one of them and I won't complain."

Cooper's eyes sparkled. "But they wouldn't taste nearly as good straight from the bag. It's a matter of ambience, you see. It's like ordering filet mignon in a deluxe restaurant versus microwaving a hamburger at home. They're both beef, but what a difference." He sniffed her wrist. "Speaking of ambience—have you stopped using Isobel's perfume?"

She frowned. "No—because I never used Isobel's perfume. Do you mean I smell like her?"

The corner of his mouth twitched as if he wanted to

smile. "I wouldn't have put it quite so crudely, but yes. You used to, at any rate."

Hannah sighed, remembering the way that simply moving Isobel's possessions had stirred up her scent. "Her perfume permeated everything in her condo—including, apparently, my clothes. I must have gotten so used to it I couldn't smell it on myself."

"See? I told you there would be advantages to living up here instead." He pushed the sleeve of her jacket up an inch and kissed the pulse point in her wrist. "You'll get your senses back."

If he keeps this up, Hannah thought, *I'm far more likely to lose them altogether...*

The butler tapped on the door and pushed it halfway open. "Sir, the doorman is here, and he seems to have a bit of a problem on his hands."

"Daniel?" Hannah seized the chance to stand up, but she resisted the urge to rub her palms down the sides of her skirt. "I wonder what he wants."

Something banged against the door, pushing it back against the wall, and a small, furry whirlwind flew through and made a beeline for Hannah. "Brutus?" she said blankly.

The pug didn't pause till he'd circled her three times, wrapping the leash he was dragging around her ankles like a set of shackles. Then he tried to leap up into her arms, but since most of the leash was tangled around her feet, he could jump only a few inches. The best he could do was to thud against her knees, knocking Hannah over before he slid down in a heap on the floor.

Cooper caught her, breaking her fall and lowering her till she was sitting on the couch once more.

Five seconds later the doorman appeared, out of breath.

"Sorry," he managed. "It was like he could sniff you out, Ms. Lowe, and once he got the direction he was gone."

"I hope this means that you're taking over the dog-walking duties," Cooper said flatly.

"Not me." Daniel sounded horrified. "Mrs. Patterson started having trouble breathing, and the ambulance crew just took her to the hospital. She asked me to bring the mutt to you, Ms. Lowe. She said it would relieve her mind to know he was all right. I didn't have the heart to tell her you'd moved up here. So—what do I do with him now?"

The words were out before Cooper could stop himself. "Call the animal pound."

Brutus had planted both front paws on Hannah's knees and was trying to stretch himself out so he could lick her face, but at the sound of Cooper's voice the pug eyed him and growled softly.

"Not good diplomacy," Hannah advised. She reached out to stroke the wrinkles on the dog's forehead.

"What? The pound?"

"No," she said, sounding as if she was trying very hard to be patient. "I was advising Brutus not to growl at you, under the circumstances. Did you bring up his crate, Daniel?"

"It's in the hallway, Miss."

"Then Abbott will show you where to put it."

Cooper muttered, "My first choice would be on the fire escape. *Hanging* from the fire escape. And don't bother with the crate, Abbott, just use the leash."

Hannah rolled her eyes. "Come on, Cooper. As big as this place is, you'll never know he's here. Besides, how would you like the story to get around that a little dog like this one can put a big, strong guy like you on the run? Abbott, perhaps there's a corner in the kitchen?"

Without a word, the butler backed out of the room, and the doorman followed.

Brutus managed to get enough of his leash free to let him climb up onto Hannah's lap, where he lolled, stared at Cooper and sneered.

Or at least that was what it looked like to Cooper. He felt like making faces right back at the pug.

If the vile little animal had planned this interruption, Cooper thought irritably, he couldn't have done a better job. The moment he'd had been getting somewhere... And he had been making progress, though Hannah might deny it with her last breath. He'd felt the tremor that had run through her as he'd traced her lifeline with his tongue. He'd intended to take it slow but steady, to press home the advantage that he'd gained...

Instead, here they sat, with a good three feet of space and a dog between them. Brutus wriggled round in Hannah's lap, sniffed her hand, glared at Cooper, and began to industriously lick her fingers as if he was intent on removing Cooper's scent.

"That's adding insult to injury," Cooper told the animal. "If you had any brain at all, you foolish animal, you'd be cowering and begging me not to throw you out in the cold." Brutus stopped licking long enough to grin at him.

Hannah untangled the leash from around her ankles—very nice, shapely ankles, Cooper noted—and put the dog on the floor. Brutus began sniffing his way around the coffee table.

"There's got to be more to it than that," Hannah said.

"More to what? If you're suggesting that we pick up where we left off, I'm warning you—I'm not kissing any part of you that the dog has. Though, come to think of it, that leaves plenty of interesting territory."

A tinge of pink rose in her cheeks. "I wasn't talking about anything of the sort. I meant that it's a bit odd, if your mother's so sensitive about Ken Stephens, that she doesn't seem to resent me because I happened to end up owning the Lovers' Box."

"Or even," Cooper added calmly, "because you're withholding her property in order to blackmail me."

She ignored him. "Therefore, it's reasonable to conclude that she's got more against my boss than just his job. What about your father?"

"How did my father get dragged into this?"

"I just wondered if Ken could have done something to him that would have inspired your mother to resent him."

Cooper shook his head. "My father has been out of the picture for years—and toward the end of the marriage, Mother wouldn't have resented any insult to him, she'd probably have applauded it."

Hannah wrinkled her nose. "Your parents were divorced? Ken wasn't his attorney, by any chance?"

Cooper hadn't realized till just then how very cute that little nose of hers was. Now if she'd just keep it out of things that didn't concern her... "You really are grasping at straws, Hannah. Believe me, it's Isobel that Mother's annoyed about. And as for her not being resentful about the Lovers' Box, it would be interesting to see what she had to say about it if anybody in the family was planning a wedding."

"You mean she really believes that not having the Lovers' Box can jinx a marriage?"

"My parents' divorce was the first in the family."

"But not the first unsuccessful marriage. Take your grandparents—"

"They stayed married till the day he died."

"That's not what I call successful."

"It's all in the definition. Call me unsentimental, but I imagine a good many of those supposedly happy couples stuck together for years only because there weren't any other workable options."

"You're not just unsentimental, Cooper, you're a cynic. I bet you think if Adam and Eve had had legal counsel, they'd have battled it out over who got the tax deduction for losing the Garden of Eden."

"That's what made it Paradise—the fact that there wasn't a lawyer within sight."

She stuck her tongue out at him. Cooper could think of several fun ways to retaliate—if it hadn't been for the dog. He reached for the chips, but Brutus had tugged the bag onto the floor. The pug took his nose out of the cellophane just long enough to growl at Cooper's outstretched hand.

"Fine, old boy. You can have 'em all."

"No, he can't—they'll make him sick." Hannah rescued the chip bag and put it back on the coffee table. "Come on, Brutus. It's past your bedtime—and mine, too."

The pug backed away from her outstretched hand, retreating so far under a chair that only his rubbery black nose was visible.

Hannah put her hands on her hips. "Don't make me come down there after you," she ordered.

"There's an easier way," Cooper said lazily.

"Really? You've suddenly become an animal psychologist?"

"No, but I understand how this particular mutt's mind works." He cupped Hannah's face in his hands and let his thumbs slowly trace the disbelieving curve of her eyebrows. "All I have to do is kiss you, and Brutus will come out from hiding to bite my ankle."

"And then what? You kick him across the room?" She sounded a little breathless.

"I'll get to that," Cooper murmured. "First things first." He bent his head. "I just hope you appreciate the sacrifice I'm making here—letting myself be bitten to save you a little trouble."

She opened her mouth to argue, so instead of kissing her, Cooper settled for nibbling at her lower lip. There was no hurry, after all. He'd be happy to do this all night—to tease, caress, nuzzle... His goal was a simple one—a playful embrace that would entice her into wanting more.

But the first flicker of Hannah's response set off a primeval hunger deep inside him, and abruptly he realized that not even her surrender could entirely satisfy him now. The only thing which would slake his desire would be for her to admit to a need every bit as great as his own.

But in the meantime, he thought fuzzily, he'd take whatever he could get...

Unfortunately, it wasn't going to be much; Hannah was pushing him away, and reluctantly he released her.

"Yes, indeed," she said dryly. "That was quite a sacrifice. Now I know exactly how it feels to be a lamb led to the slaughter." She was gone before he could answer.

A soft whine at his feet made Cooper look down, and a wave of unholy glee swept over him at the sight of Brutus with his head firmly stuck inside the now-empty corn chip bag.

It wasn't the dog's plight which amused him, however, or even the sudden realization that when it came right down to a choice, Brutus had preferred to chew on illicit corn chips instead of his ankle.

What was tickling Cooper as he stooped to rescue the pug was the knowledge that despite her cool exterior, Hannah had been a lot more shaken by that kiss than she'd wanted to admit. If she'd really been as self-possessed as she'd pretended to be, she wouldn't have forgotten about Brutus.

He was making progress after all, Cooper told himself. And not only with Hannah. At this rate, he might even be able to negotiate a compromise with the dog.

With one eye on the computer screen and the other on the open doorway of her cubicle, Hannah logged on to the Internet and checked her mail. There were no answers yet from the headhunters' organizations she'd contacted—which should have been no surprise, since she'd sent her queries out just the day before.

It only feels like it's been weeks, she thought.

And no wonder. If Cooper kept up the kind of pressure he'd been applying last night…

Then she'd just have to remain unmoved. And how difficult could that be, when—as he had last night—Cooper himself would remind her with every gesture and every touch that he wasn't taking the game seriously?

Very difficult, she admitted. Just remembering the way he had kissed her last night was enough to set her pulses skittering once more…

Of course, dwelling on her reaction would only make it harder to deal with him next time. She'd do far better to forget last night's episode altogether, so she could start off their next encounter with a fresh slate. Yes, that was the sensible move—to put last night firmly in the past. To pretend it hadn't even happened.

There was certainly no point in speculating what approach Cooper would use next. A man who could turn a bag of corn chips into a tool of seduction could use any item that came to hand. It would be a waste of time to try to anticipate what he would do.

If she had any sense at all, instead of even thinking about him she would concentrate all her efforts on finding a new job. That way Cooper wouldn't have time to calculate his next move...

"You're thinking about him again," Hannah muttered, and with a clatter of computer keys she sent out another blizzard of résumés.

Just as the last of them was safely away, Brenton appeared at the cubicle door. He eyed the computer screen. "Doing some research? You'll have to let it wait. I have a couple of files here that must go up to Ken Stephens's office right away." He slapped the folders down on her desk.

Hannah glanced at them. "Perhaps you should brief me, in case he has questions."

"There's no need for you even to see him. Just drop the folders off."

In other words, Hannah thought, these were routine matters, something that any of the secretaries could have delivered, if interoffice mail wasn't quick enough.

She kept her voice pleasant. "I didn't realize you'd added messenger girl to my job description, Brenton."

His eyes narrowed. "And I didn't realize you'd added insolence to your qualifications." He turned on his heel and strode away.

Hannah picked up the folders and climbed the stairs to the executive floor.

Ken Stephens's office door was closed, and no one was at the secretary's desk. Hannah bit her lip and considered her options.

Ordinarily, she'd have placed the folders squarely in the center of the secretary's blotter and gone on about her own business. The secretary should be back at any moment, and no one else was present to see the folders, much less pry into their contents. And in any case, these were ordinary papers—the most meddlesome of snoops couldn't find anything of interest here.

But the firm's rule said that nothing was ever to be left in the open. Stephens & Webster promised its clients complete confidentiality, so folders or letters or even scribbled notes were never to be left where they might be seen by someone who wasn't directly involved in the case.

Had Brenton set her up?

She couldn't help but be suspicious. She could think of no other reason for him to send her upstairs on this mundane errand.

You're becoming paranoid, she told herself. Leaving that box of Jacob Jones's papers in Cooper's car had been a much more flagrant violation of the rule, but Brenton hadn't made nearly as much of a fuss about it as she'd expected he would.

Unless he'd simply laid low until another opportunity presented itself—until he'd found a way to get rid of her without having to actually do the dirty work himself.

If Hannah dropped the folders on the desk and walked away, and Ken Stephens himself popped out of his office and saw her, he'd fire her on the spot, no questions asked.

If, on the other hand, she waited for the secretary to reappear, Brenton would probably be sitting in her office counting the minutes, and he'd accuse her of dawdling, of not working to capacity, of not giving full devotion to Stephens & Webster...

Whatever happened, Hannah would end up looking bad.

From the corner of her eye, she caught a flash of movement from the hallway, and relief surged over her. If that was the secretary returning—

But it wasn't. The woman who stopped in the doorway

was obviously as startled to see Hannah as Hannah was to see her.

And she was embarrassed, too, Hannah thought with a rush of sympathy. It was bad enough for Sarah Winston to have to seek out Ken Stephens and apologize, but to run into Hannah in the process...

Ken opened the door of his office a few inches. Hannah thought she caught an almost-furtive look in his eyes, and all her suspicions of Brenton flooded back. He could have arranged for Kitty to leave her desk at the strategic time, and she wouldn't put it past him to have maneuvered Ken into appearing at the crucial instant, either.

She stepped forward and held out the folders. "I'm sorry to interrupt your conference," she said briskly, "but Brenton wanted me to deliver these straight to you, sir."

Ken looked at the folders, and then at Hannah, and his eyebrows drew together in a frown.

Hannah felt like clicking her heels together and saluting triumphantly as she turned away. Instead, she held her head high and gave Sarah an encouraging smile as she crossed the waiting room.

She wished there had been an opportunity for more. Sarah Winston might be a power in her own right in the city, but at the moment she looked more like a scared schoolgirl, in need of all the sympathy and support she could get.

Hannah wondered whose idea it had been to meet in Ken's office. Considering the humiliation he'd absorbed last night, Hannah wouldn't put it past the senior partner to demand the home-court advantage, just to get even with the woman who had so publicly insulted him.

It was apparent, she thought, that when Cooper had suggested his mother apologize, he'd had no idea how much he was asking of her. She just hoped Sarah would be all right.

CHAPTER SEVEN

THE wind had picked up as the day wore on, and by the time Hannah had walked the few blocks from the law firm to Barron's Court, she was imagining a mug of hot chocolate big enough to swim in. She was so absorbed in the fantasy that she didn't even notice Daniel the doorman trying to get her attention until it was too late to stop the elevator from closing in his face.

She thought about going back to see what he wanted, but decided that surely whatever Daniel wanted would keep for a few minutes. She'd be going out again soon in order to walk the dog, anyway.

The mere thought of facing the wind once more sent a shiver up Hannah's spine. But she couldn't disappoint Brutus again; the pug had looked at her so reproachfully that morning that Hannah was still feeling guilty. She ought to be ashamed of herself, he'd seemed to be saying, for actually abandoning him last night—and to his sworn enemy, of all people.

It had been pretty silly of her to cut and run like that, she thought. Letting Cooper see that he was getting to her was a big mistake. If she'd only been able to maintain her presence of mind for a couple of minutes longer...

When she reached the penthouse, the first thing Hannah heard was a light, feminine laugh coming from the big living room, and suddenly Daniel's frantic attempt to intercept her made sense. Gentleman that he was, she thought with a smile, he'd been trying to keep her from being hurt by catching Cooper with another woman, right in her own new home.

It was a sweet gesture, even though it was a misguided one. As if she would care who Cooper entertained!

She waved casually at the pair sitting by the huge windows overlooking the city, and she would have simply gone off to change her clothes if Cooper hadn't called her name. Curiosity drew her back to the living room. Had it really been a note of desperation she'd heard in his voice?

"Kitty dropped in to see you," Cooper said. He reached out to catch Hannah's hand and pull her close.

Under the urgent pressure of his grip, she could do nothing but take the hint, perching on the arm of his overstuffed chair. Definitely it had been desperation in his voice, she thought. "I told you so," she said softly.

The woman sitting across from him gave Hannah a brilliant smile. "I'm so glad you've come, Hannah."

As if, Hannah thought, *she's the hostess and I'm the drop-in company!*

"I wanted to ask you about the condo downstairs," Kitty confided. "The one you used to live in."

"How thoughtful it was of you not to take up my valuable time at work with such personal questions," Hannah said sweetly.

Kitty looked horrified. "Oh, no, Daddy wouldn't like it at all if I did that."

So she'd just happened to drop in on Cooper instead... The woman was nearly as transparent as a mirror. Unfortunately, that didn't make the menace any easier to deal with.

"I'm thinking of asking him to buy it for me," Kitty went on. "The condo, I mean. I've always liked Barron's Court. But I wanted to ask you if there was anything I should know about it first, before I make up my mind."

"I should think the building manager would be the one to answer those questions." Hannah tried to slide off the arm of the chair, but Cooper's arm clamped around her waist and prevented her from moving.

"I was just going to walk the dog," she protested. "He's probably dying for some exercise."

"No, he's not. He's out for a run right now. And before you start getting suspicious—no, I did not throw him off the balcony. I didn't even turn him loose in front of the building. Abbott took him out. So you may as well relax and enjoy your guest."

He was still holding her fast. His hand intimately cupped her hipbone, and the heat of his fingers seemed to burn through the lightweight wool of her skirt. Hannah stretched an arm across his shoulders in what was intended to look like a loving gesture. The pinch she administered to the back of his neck, however, was anything but tender. Cooper started to yelp, then turned the sound into a cough.

"That's not the kind of information I need," Kitty said. "Daddy will take care of all those little things."

Little things, Hannah deduced, like purchase prices and condo fees and insurance and mortgages.

"But since you lived there, you can tell me…well, if there's anything strange about the place."

Strange? Somehow, Hannah thought that Kitty wouldn't be particularly interested in the unit's quirky plumbing or the fact that the kitchen light switch had been put in upside down and never corrected. "Well, I doubt Isobel's ghost is still hanging around now that all her belongings are gone," she said dryly.

Kitty's eyes widened. "She was there? Truly?"

Instantly, Hannah regretted the impulsive comment. Was Kitty really such an airhead that she didn't recognize irony when she heard it?

"Because it would be just too wonderful to have a ghost," Kitty said. "Especially Isobel's ghost."

"You wouldn't think so if you'd known the real woman," Cooper muttered.

Kitty ignored him. "It's such a romantic story, isn't it, Hannah?"

"I suppose your father filled you in on all the details," Cooper said.

"He wouldn't talk about a client, so I had to pick the story up here and there." Kitty sounded almost dreamy. "She adored her lover so much that she was willing to sacrifice everything for him, even though he could never marry her."

"You make it sound just like a fairy tale," Hannah said wryly.

"As far as fairy tales go," Cooper mused, "I've always wondered how well Cinderella and the prince got along afterward. Whenever she got mad, I bet she threw her glass slipper at him, and then he accused her of having no class. And take Sleeping Beauty—when she hit middle age, she probably ran away from her husband and kids in order to relive the youth she'd missed."

His voice was light, but Hannah couldn't help but wonder how many similar scenes he'd experienced for himself. Between his parents' divorce and his grandparents' troubled marriage, perhaps it was no wonder if Cooper himself preferred to steer clear of anything that smelled like commitment.

She could picture him as a little boy, and later as a young man, caught in the middle—maybe even pressured to take sides—and the image made her feel overwhelmingly sad. She doubted, however, that Cooper would welcome her sympathy, so she kept her voice casual. "Maybe Isobel had the right idea after all. The illusion must have been easier to maintain when she only had to keep it going on a part-time basis.''

Kitty sighed. ''I just think the whole story is tragically romantic. Sort of like Romeo and Juliet.''

Hannah heard Cooper's smothered snicker, but she didn't dare look at him or she'd have burst out laughing herself. She knew only too well what he was thinking, because she, too, was trying to picture his grandfather—Irving of the receding hairline and pot belly—as a romantic hero. And then there was Isobel; try as she might, Hannah couldn't imagine the woman she'd known killing herself for love.

Kitty looked curiously from one of them to the other.

The doorbell rang, and Cooper shifted in his chair. ''I should see who that is,'' he began.

''Don't even think about disappearing,'' Hannah said through gritted teeth.

Before he could get up, however, Abbott came down the hall. Behind him, almost as close as a shadow, was Brutus, still panting from his run.

''Come here, buddy,'' Hannah called, and the pug made a hard left turn into the living room, strode past her without a second look, and pawed at Cooper's knee. Cooper patted the chair cushion beside him and the pug leaped up, turned round, and settled in.

Hannah's jaw dropped. ''Brutus, you traitor!''

''Well-named, isn't he?'' Cooper murmured.

The dog grinned.

She glared at Cooper. ''How did you do that?''

Cooper shrugged. ''We had a little man-to-dog talk last night.'' He looked past Abbott to the woman at the door. ''Come on in, Mother.''

Sarah paused between foyer and living room. ''I was in

the neighborhood, but I don't mean to interrupt if you're entertaining.''

"Not at all," Cooper said cheerfully. "Kitty just stopped by for a couple of minutes to ask a question.''

Even Kitty, Hannah noted, had trouble ignoring the heavy hint that it was time to leave; she scowled at Cooper for a moment before she remembered herself and smiled brightly once more. "I don't have to hurry away.''

"She says," Cooper went on, "that she's interested in buying the condo downstairs.''

"Really?" Sarah said. "That's where I'm headed myself, to see how much work we'll need to do before putting it on the market. If you want to take a look, Kitty, come along with me." Almost briskly, she herded Kitty toward the door, stopping in the foyer to add, "That little matter we talked about last night, Cooper? It's been handled. We can discuss all the details later.''

Kitty was still protesting faintly as they went out.

"I guess that's that," Hannah said as the door closed behind them. She slid off the arm of Cooper's chair and went to straighten an arrangement of calla lilies on a nearby table. "And you tried to tell me you didn't need protecting from Kitty.''

"She trapped me in the elevator," Cooper protested.

"I did warn you not to underestimate her. Anyone who's that single-minded can be as hard to deflect as a bulldozer. I just hope you appreciate how your mother dislodged her.''

Cooper leaned back in his chair. "Of course I do. Bless my mother—always willing to sacrifice herself for me. You'd have thought, the way she swept Kitty out of here, that she believed Kitty was actually interested.''

"And that she was ready to deal with Ken Stephens,''

Hannah mused. "Which I'd say is doubtful, judging by how she looked today when she was apologizing to him."

"I thought that must be what she was talking about." Cooper didn't sound particularly interested.

Hannah was annoyed. If he'd seen Sarah's face today in Ken's office, he wouldn't have treated the matter so offhandedly. In fact, Sarah had still looked a bit pale tonight, as if she hadn't entirely recovered from whatever Ken had said to her.

That's none of your business, Hannah told herself. *It's not like you're really involved in this family—you're just pretending to be.*

And why she should feel a wave of sadness at the idea...well, that was obvious. Under other circumstances, she could see herself and Sarah being friends, so of course she was concerned about the woman's feelings.

It certainly had nothing to do with Cooper.

She tipped her head to one side to study the new lines of the flower arrangement. "By the way," she said casually, "that was quite a nice pass Kitty made at you."

Cooper frowned.

"You mean you actually didn't recognize it? Perhaps the lady's slightly more subtle than a bulldozer after all." Hannah gave a last tug to a calla lily. "Now that I think about it, though, I'm not certain whether she was actually picturing an affair or only seeing herself in the role of a tragic heroine."

"You mean all that nonsense about how romantic Isobel's life was?"

Hannah nodded. "And even setting herself up in the condo downstairs so whenever you get tired of me she'll be handy. I thought that was a really nice touch."

"As if I'd find anything romantic about that specific location," Cooper grumbled.

"Well, you can't expect Kitty to comprehend all the fine points. But you might want to consider your defense system for after I'm gone, because your mother can't be here to protect you all the time, either. And let's face it, Cooper—cornering you in the elevator today might have been a lucky accident, but Kitty's only going to get better with practice."

"And you had to go tell her a tale about Isobel's ghost. Why you thought that was a good idea—"

"I was trying to help. I expected she'd scream and run, not find the idea an inducement. But hey—look on the positive side. Every evening that she's holding a seance in order to entice Isobel to come back is an evening she won't be bothering you."

"I'll try to keep that in mind," Cooper said dryly. "How is your job search going?"

"What you're really asking is how long you'll have to get your strategy in place, right? Poor guy," Hannah mocked. "On the one hand you can't wait to get me out of your hair, but as soon as I leave, Kitty will have the playing field all to herself. Talk about having mixed feelings!"

"Enjoying this, aren't you, Hannah?"

"Watching you struggling to get out of a pickle? It has its moments. At any rate, don't panic just yet—because nobody's made me an offer at all, much less one I can feel passionate about."

Cooper grinned, and Hannah felt hot color surge over her. When, she asked herself irritably, would she learn to watch every word when he was around? What was there about this man that made her forget every precaution she'd learned in law school?

"Oh, well," he said lazily, "since you've brought up the subject—"

"Job offer. I was talking of job offers I could feel enthusiastic about."

"But I wasn't." He came up behind her and rested his hands on her shoulders, his thumbs moving in slow circles. "Your neck muscles are stretched tight," he said. "So don't try to tell me you're not tense. How long are you going to deny what you want, Hannah?"

"I don't want you."

Amusement warmed his voice. "We both know better than that." His lips came to rest against the nape of her neck, and a tingle slowly spread out from the point of contact till it had engulfed Hannah's entire body.

"If you're asking when I plan to give in to your seductive games," she said as firmly as she could, "the answer is, about the same time hell freezes over."

The massage didn't even slow. "Good." The barely whispered word tickled her sensitive skin.

Hannah tried to look over her shoulder. "What do you mean, *good?* I thought I was making it painfully clear that—"

"Because you've finally put a counteroffer on the table," Cooper murmured. "Now we can start to negotiate."

A dull, gray autumn rain was falling, bringing evening on even earlier than normal, when Cooper stopped his car directly in front of Stephens & Webster. Hannah was waiting for him under the awning, and he pushed the passenger door open so she could duck inside.

As she slammed the door, he draped an arm across her shoulders and felt the chilly dampness of her raincoat seeping through the sleeve of his jacket. "Sorry I'm late," he said. "Here, let me make it up by getting you warm in a hurry." He pulled her close.

Hannah planted a hand against his chest and pushed.

"There's no need for a demonstration. Nobody can see into the car in this rain anyway, and Brenton went home an hour ago so there's no one to perform for."

"I'd have sworn I saw him skulking around the building," Cooper argued. But he let go of her and put the Ferrari into gear. "You know, Hannah, it's been a whole week now since we agreed to negotiate—"

Hannah's lips tightened. Cooper amused himself by speculating how long it would take to kiss them soft again.

At the rate he was going, he admitted ruefully, it would probably take a couple of months even to work his way up to a good try.

Hannah pointed out, "You mean, since you unilaterally declared we were going to negotiate."

He decided not to argue the point. "And I'm not getting anywhere."

"Noticed that, did you? It's amazing how perceptive you can be sometimes."

She settled back against the door, as far as possible from him, and watched the street. The hiss of tires on the wet pavement and the soft swish of the wipers were the only sound in the car.

When the car pulled up in front of the main entrance to Barron's Court, Daniel the doorman strode hastily out to the curb with an oversize umbrella to shield Hannah as she got out of the car. She went without a backward look, and Cooper took the car around to the garage rather than wait for one of the valets to return.

That kind of avoidance—sitting as far away from him as she could, refusing to look at him, not initiating conversations—provided the only positive note Cooper had been able to find lately. If she really was as indifferent as she'd like him to think, she wouldn't be trying so hard to stay out of his way.

Or was that just wishful thinking?

As he came into the lobby from the back way, he was trying to figure out what else Hannah might have on her mind, and he almost walked straight past his mother without seeing her. He checked at the last minute, paused to summon the elevator, and said, "Come on up for a drink, Mother. Hannah should already be..." He took a closer look at the contents of the shopping bag she carried and added suspiciously, "You had better not be conspiring with Hannah to redecorate my penthouse again."

"Of course not," Sarah said flatly. "I have much more sense than that."

He wasn't convinced. "Then why are you carrying a bag full of fabric scraps?"

"They're not scraps, they're upholstery and drapery samples." The elevator arrived, and Sarah stepped in and pushed the button for the seventh floor.

Cooper noted the floor she'd chosen. "I wouldn't advise redecorating Isobel's condo before you put it up for sale, Mother. Clean the carpets, yes, but you won't get the money back out of the extras."

"It's not Isobel's anymore." Sarah held her head up a little straighter. "It's Kitty's now."

"She actually bought it? I thought the whole idea was just an excuse to hang around Barron's Court." Cooper was feeling a little seasick. "So if the deal's done, what are you doing? This looks like you're going back into the interior decorating business."

"She liked the ideas I had, and she wanted to see more." But Sarah didn't have quite as much self-control as she'd like, Cooper noted, because she had colored just a little.

Before he could find his voice, the elevator door opened and he stepped forward automatically to hold it for his mother. He reached for her arm, but Sarah shook her head. "Don't make a big thing of it, Cooper. Isobel's gone, and it's time to let the past fade."

He shook his head in confusion. It was an astounding statement, coming from the same woman who just over a week ago had flatly refused to let the past fade, instead declaring a very public war against Ken Stephens....

Just as the elevator started up once more, he caught a glimpse of the front entrance of Kitty's new condo as the door opened and his mother hurried across the hall. His jaw was still slack when he reached the top floor.

Upstairs in the penthouse, Hannah stood in the center of the foyer, both her hands upraised as she tried to restore order to her hair. Cooper watched with appreciation as she poked hairpins in at random to create a makeshift French twist. Brutus stopped jitterbugging in circles around her and turned his attention to Cooper instead, sniffing suspiciously at his shoes.

"What's the matter with you?" Hannah asked. "Did you run into Isobel's ghost in the stairwell?"

"Isobel's ghost would have been less puzzling than what I just saw." He told her about his encounter with his mother. "And the oddest thing of all—guess who greeted her."

"You mean it wasn't Kitty?"

"Kitty was there. I heard her voice. But it was Ken Stephens who opened the door."

Hannah bit her lip.

"I know," Cooper said. "It doesn't make any sense at all."

She sighed. "Or maybe it does. I thought, when I saw your mother in Ken's office and later that day when she was here, that she looked odd. If the apology had been the end of it, she'd have been relieved. Instead, she was still obviously stressed. And that was the day she practically dragged Kitty out of here to go and look at Isobel's condo.''

''You mean that maybe she wasn't simply protecting me after all.'' Cooper shook his head. ''It's too silly to think about, Hannah. You're implying that Ken's blackmailing her, but using extortion techniques to make her sell him an apartment—''

''Didn't I tell you that what Kitty wants she generally gets? Anyway, maybe we're overreacting. Maybe it's not blackmail, maybe they just made a deal. Sarah insulted him pretty publicly—so helping his daughter to get settled would be a way to make it clear, also very publicly, that she'd been wrong. I think she'd rather do that than—say—go to the bar association banquet with Ken this weekend.'' She gave up on restoring her French twist and began pulling out pins instead. ''The banquet would be even more public, and it would raise even more eyebrows.''

Cooper wasn't listening; his fingers itched to help. He longed to search out the remaining pins, to rake his hands gently through the chestnut waves, to bury his face in the softness of the unruly mass.

And that was only the beginning of what he wanted to do.

Blackmail... The word echoed strangely in his mind. He'd told Hannah he wouldn't blackmail her into his bed. At the time he'd been certain he wouldn't need to.

But this was all taking far longer than he'd imagined it could. And he had to admit that after ten days of unsuccessful persuasion, the whole idea of blackmail was starting to look awfully attractive.

Why, Hannah asked herself, hadn't she told him?

There had been opportunities enough—in the car on the

ride home, over dinner, all through the evening. But each time she had braced herself to bring up the subject, something had intervened and kept her from speaking. Traffic had been too heavy for him to give her his full attention, or Abbott had come in with the next course, or he'd gotten a call about work...

And so she hadn't told Cooper that after a week of searching, sending résumés, and talking to prospective employers on the telephone, she had received a job offer. All she had to do was say the word, and all of this would be over.

No more worry about Brenton's scheming. No more uncertainty about her future. No more exploiting the Lovers' Box. No more feeling guilty for not giving it back to Cooper—or to Sarah—right away.

So why hadn't she grabbed the job? Why had she temporized and asked for time to think about it? Why had she requested a chance to fly out and look at the firm before giving her answer?

It would be a big change, that was certain. Not only a new job and a new firm, but a new city and even a new state. Still, she'd moved before; it wasn't as if she had exactly set roots here.

Since she was moving across state lines, she'd have to study for another bar exam. But she had few doubts about passing; the ones she'd already taken were the toughest in the nation.

It made sense to be cautious, of course, and to go and look things over for herself before making a final choice. It even made sense to arrange the timing of her visit in such a way that Brenton couldn't guess her intentions before she was ready to announce them.

But none of those very good reasons explained why she hadn't told Cooper about the offer.

Unable to sleep, Hannah pushed back her blankets and tiptoed down the hall toward the kitchen. The penthouse was silent, except for Brutus rustling in his crate in the corner and the sonorous tick of the grandfather clock in the library as the hands inched past two o'clock in the morning.

She raided the cupboard for a package of crackers, and she was pouring a tall glass of milk when Cooper spoke from the doorway. "If this is a come-as-you-are party," he said, "I think I'm overdressed."

Startled, Hannah jerked, and she almost dropped the milk pitcher. Slowly she turned to face him.

It was obvious what he meant by being overdressed; her flannel pajamas, thick as the fabric was, felt like nothing at all compared to his jeans and sweater. "I thought you were asleep," she said.

He shook his head. "I haven't been sleeping well lately, so I hadn't bothered to go to bed yet. When I heard a little rustle in the hallway, I thought I'd see what kind of creature was stirring."

Hannah's heart seemed to be doing a gymnastic routine. Carefully, she set the milk back into the refrigerator. *Tell him,* she ordered herself. *He'll be as relieved as you are.*

She reminded herself of all the reasons she was glad the farce was coming to an end—all the reasons that Cooper, too, would be relieved.

No more people to convince, she thought. No more roles to play. No more pretending to be in love with him...

But then, you haven't been pretending, have you, Hannah?

She stared across the kitchen at Cooper, tall and lean...and very dangerous. Dangerous because of the way he affected her. Because of the way she reacted to him.

Because she loved him.

The soft whisper of truth struck Hannah like a whip.

Now it was all clear. It would have been only sensible, on the day when the Lovers' Box had come into his hands, to have simply accepted his offer and given it back to him. But she hadn't. She'd probed for the story, for every detail and nuance.

Not because she'd cared about the box, she admitted, or even particularly about the story. She'd done it because she cared about him. She'd hung on to the box—because she wanted to hang on to him.

When, she asked herself, had she passed over the line from public pretense into private fervor? When had her reluctant fondness for a man who was a bit of a rogue turned to heart-shattering love?

CHAPTER EIGHT

HANNAH felt dizzy. The truth she had tried so hard not to see had sliced through her heart like the beam of a laser. Now there was no going back; she would never again be able to deny how she felt about Cooper.

She didn't know exactly when irritation had become fascination. When he'd charmed the dog? When he'd stopped being the sophisticate and admitted—though not in so many words—that he could use a little help in holding Kitty at arm's length? Or even before that?

She'd always felt discomfort when he was near—but had that been awareness and desire, rather than the dislike she'd thought it was? Was that why she'd been so touchy when he was around, and why it had been so difficult to guard her tongue?

She had no idea. In any case, she supposed it didn't matter, for thinking about the whys and whens was only another tool of distraction. Another way to keep from thinking about the only important question which was left.

What was she going to do about it?

Nothing, the sensible half of her brain argued. There was nothing she could do. They had agreed to their terms, and it wasn't within her power to change the rules of the game just because she'd suddenly gotten a shock. Because she'd allowed herself to be foolish enough to fall in love with him.

Without question, Cooper was holding up his end of the bargain. No one in the city, with the possible exception of his mother, had the slightest doubt that they were lovers. And that was exactly what she'd asked of him.

In return, Hannah would have to keep her word. As soon as she'd settled on a new job, she would return the Lovers' Box to him, and the deal would be complete.

And she would likely never see him again.

The realization clutched at her throat, threatening to choke her. Once she had looked forward to a time when she need not encounter him. Now it seemed like the cruelest of all possible punishments.

Suddenly her reluctance to take the job she'd been offered, or even to tell him about it, made sense. Suddenly she knew why she'd felt no rush to check out the new job, the new city, the new state. Her concern about Brenton's manipulative pressure was outweighed by the urge to delay. The longer she could put off a decision, the longer she could pretend that she would never have to leave Cooper.

And, she admitted, she could also pretend that Cooper didn't want her to go.

That fantasy, like her love for him, had crept up on her so quietly that Hannah had been unaware of how it had invaded and colored her every thought. Now she faced the challenge of rooting it out, of destroying the fantasy before it could destroy her.

She knew that the more quickly she acted, the less it would hurt and the better the results would be. Still, she cringed away from the thought. And, she reminded herself, even if this turned out to be the perfect job offer, there were practical limitations on how quickly she could move to accept it. She'd still have to give a month's notice before leaving Stephens & Webster...

If she had needed confirmation of her feelings, she would have found it in the wave of relief which surged over her at the thought of having a few more days—maybe even weeks—with him.

In that length of time, anything might happen....

Abruptly, she realized that Cooper was watching her with obvious curiosity, and she caught herself up short. Did the expression on her face tell of the stunning discovery she'd made? Could those quicksilver eyes look straight into her soul?

Deliberately, she raised her glass and drank half her milk. When she set it down again, she said, without looking straight at him, "I suppose you're thinking up another way to pressure me to go to bed with you."

His voice was almost gruff. "As a matter of fact, I was simply enjoying the view. But if you want me to use a little persuasion—"

He didn't even move, but suddenly Hannah's heart was pounding as if he were looming over her.

What, exactly, did she want?

Cooper had left no doubt about his desires. If she wanted to make love with him, all she had to do was say the word.

As if he'd read her mind, he said, "If you want me to use a little persuasion—or more than a little—maybe you should think about why. If you sleep with me, Hannah, there'll be no crying foul in the morning. No pretending that you were forced, or pushed, or even swept off your feet."

That's not fair, she thought. *Even though I sort of asked for it.*

How foolish could she be, even to consider tossing herself over the precipice? It was bad enough to have to admit that she'd fallen in love with a man who was interested in her only as a conquest. To fling herself headlong into an affair—to reduce herself to a notch on Cooper Winston's bedpost—would be suicidal.

And yet...

Would it be such a horrible thing to do, to express her love in a physical way even though she knew the intensity of her feelings was not returned? To enjoy the satisfaction she could have, even though she knew that the intimacy they would share would be no more than a shadow of what she wanted?

There was her answer, of course. She faced it with something close to reluctance, but she knew in her battered heart that a poor substitute would be worse than nothing at all.

He obviously saw the decision in her face, and the corner of his mouth twisted as if in regret. "On the other hand," he said almost wryly, "if a little more gentle persuasion right now would be enough to tip the scales, I suppose I could force myself to ignore my conscience and—"

She shook her head. "Your conscience has nothing to do with this, Cooper. You thought you'd already done all the convincing that was necessary, so you could safely stand back and pretend to let me have a free choice and still get precisely what you wanted."

"On the contrary. My mother raised me to be a gentleman."

"I'm sure she *tried*," Hannah said dryly.

"You're a hard woman, Hannah Lowe. Which reminds me—I've been thinking about the Lovers' Box lately."

Hannah paused in midstep, then went on across the kitchen to rinse her glass. "Would you care to be more specific? Do you mean you've been thinking about it more than usual, or in a different way?"

"Both. I'd like to see it."

"Why? You surely haven't forgotten what it looks like. And as I told you, it's safely locked up."

"But I have only your word for that." He shifted his position, leaning against the cabinets with his arms folded across his chest. "You say you put it in a bank vault, but you won't even say which bank. It occurred to me that I've been taking a great deal on faith. For all I know, you could have had a fit of rage after you left the restaurant that day and thrown the box in the nearest garbage can instead of taking it to the bank."

Irritated, she wheeled to face him, the glass still in her hand. "And then flat-out lied about what I'd done?"

Cooper was cautiously eyeing the glass. "You're very good at throwing things," he pointed out.

Hannah forced herself to laugh as she put the glass safely in the dishwasher, but there wasn't much humor in the sound.

"Or perhaps it's something in between—you didn't destroy it, but you have a reason to keep it hidden away. Perhaps you threw it, then changed your mind and retrieved it—but it's damaged."

Hannah shrugged. "In either case, it would be impossible to hide the facts forever. So what would be the point of trying?"

"Because, by the time you've agreed to bring the box out of hiding," Cooper said softly, "you'll already have everything you demanded from this deal."

Aghast that he could possibly think her so cunning, so calculating, Hannah simply looked at him.

"And I couldn't do anything about it. Oh, I suppose I could go tell Brenton it was all a joke, but even that wouldn't do you any harm if you were already safely away from him. You could have all the benefits of this deal and none of the costs."

"I know what a bargain is." Her voice was tight. "And I keep my word."

"Of course, at that point you could even accuse the bank of losing the box, or damaging it, and you could duck the responsibility entirely."

"Go ahead and say what you're thinking," Hannah said coolly. "You're expecting me to act the way you think Isobel would have—aren't you?"

"Isobel wouldn't have admitted there were two sides to the bargain. No, I'm not comparing you to her…exactly. Let's say instead that I may have been somewhat naive about the whole business. If the box turns out to be damaged or missing, I'll have nothing to show for my efforts."

"Trust me," Hannah said curtly. "It's in perfect condition."

"I'm glad to hear it. But I'd still like to see the box for myself."

"I'll think about arranging a field trip for you." She started to edge past him.

He didn't move out of the doorway. Instead he reached out and draped an arm across her shoulders, pulling her against his chest. Startled, Hannah looked up at him, and Cooper bent his head.

His kiss was long and slow and deep, and by the time he was finished Hannah couldn't have spelled *persuasion,* much less held out against it.

"There," he said, and released her. "Now you have two things to think about."

Cooper tugged at his bow tie and impatiently straightened the pristine white cuffs of his formal shirt. Not that he was in any particular hurry; if Hannah wanted to take the rest of the night to finish dressing it would be just fine with him.

Flaunting their supposed affair at the bar association's annual banquet had been Hannah's idea, not his—and how he'd managed to commit himself to yet another evening full of meaningless drivel was beyond him. Even worse, in his opinion, she'd accepted a date for drinks beforehand at Ken Stephens's apartment.

It was one thing, Cooper told himself, to have to stand by idly while his mother dealt with the man's demands, for Sarah was a grown woman who had long since made it clear that she wouldn't put up with interference from her son. But for Cooper, having to make polite conversation with the man who was trying—apparently with some success—to blackmail his mother was another thing altogether.

From Hannah's point of view, of course, the occasion was perfectly sensible. Making her entrance into the banquet hall not only on Cooper's arm but in the company of the senior partner would certainly dampen any further plans Brenton Bannister might have for creating trouble.

Cooper stopped pacing the foyer when he heard the soft click of a door opening down the hall, followed by the swish of fabric and the patter of quick footsteps.

Hannah came around the corner into the foyer, both hands raised to her earlobe so she could finish adjusting a crystal earring.

He'd seen her wearing tailored suits, shapeless sweats, oversize pajamas—and she'd been appealing in them all. Even the most unfeminine of garb had hinted at soft curves and interesting hollows and given him plenty to think about.

But Cooper's quite-active imagination hadn't fully anticipated the reality of Hannah in a sleeveless, figure-skimming dress made of some shiny dark green fabric, with a neckline which plunged almost to indecency and a slit up the side of the skirt which gave a flash of slender thigh with each step.

"Sorry to be running late." She held out a brief jacket which matched the dress and turned round so he could help her into it. "Mrs. Patterson finally got home this afternoon from the convalescent home, so I took Brutus back to her."

She slid into the jacket, and Cooper's hands came almost automatically to rest on her shoulders, against the heavy braid which decorated the collar of the jacket. Despite its weight, the garment added nothing but sleeves to the basic decency of the dress; just looking over Hannah's shoulder made Cooper feel a little light-headed.

She scooped her artistically tumbled hair away from her neck to rest outside the jacket's collar, and one lock curved carelessly down into the open neckline, caressing her throat and the top swell of her breast. Cooper's fingers itched to trace its path.

"If your goal is to keep me from noticing dull speakers, rubbery chicken, and soggy green beans," he said, "you've hit the answer."

"Oh?" She didn't seem to understand.

"If you must go to a party wearing something that looks like a nightgown—"

Her eyes were wide. "Oh, no," she said earnestly. "My nightgowns are much less revealing than this. But if it bothers you, just keep your eyes on Kitty instead. I doubt she'll mind." She swirled a black cape around her shoulders.

There were more people jammed into Ken Stephens's apartment than Cooper had expected, and nobody seemed to be paying the faintest attention to them. *Maybe being invited isn't quite the distinction that Hannah thinks it is.* Too bad they hadn't realized it in time to do something else instead. He could think of several ways he'd rather have spent the time...

He watched the seductive sway of Hannah's hips as she wriggled through the crowd on her way to greet their host, and followed.

Hannah stopped dead right in front of him, and he nearly ran into her. Almost automatically, Cooper's hands gripped her waist in order to steady both her and himself, and he looked over her shoulder to see what could have startled her so. Brenton Bannister with his arm possessively around Kitty? Cooper couldn't see why that combination should have stopped her cold.

Then he looked on beyond Brenton and Kitty to see his mother, with her back turned to them. She was standing beside Ken Stephens, and her hand was tucked into the crook of his elbow as if he didn't intend to let her get far away.

Cooper wasn't aware of making any sound whatever until Hannah swiveled round to face him. "Don't growl," she said under her breath. "There may be a perfectly reasonable explanation." She linked her arm in his and tugged him forward.

Sarah saw them coming, and it was apparent to Cooper that she tried to pull away from Ken. But she wasn't successful; he cupped his other hand over hers and held her even more tightly. "You have to do this, Sarah," the senior partner said softly.

Cooper shook off Hannah's restraining hold and stepped forward. "My mother doesn't have to do anything she doesn't want to."

Around them, the buzz of conversation diminished slightly.

Hannah's voice was low but firm. "We are not going to discuss this in public."

Cooper hadn't heard that particular note in her voice since the day she'd spoken up and cost him a cool fifteen million dollars. He hoped her tone wasn't an omen, for even though there seemed to be no money at stake just now, he hated to think what she might cost him.

Hannah pushed open a door and waved Ken and Sarah through. Cooper wondered irritably how she happened to know her way around Ken Stephens's apartment so well—until he realized that she looked as surprised as he felt to find herself in a powder room so small that there was barely room for the four of them to stand.

"It's certainly private," Cooper muttered. "You couldn't fit a housefly in here."

Ken smothered a chuckle. "I have to admit to some relief that there isn't enough room for you to take a swing at me, Cooper."

"Which must mean you think I'll have good reason to sock you in the jaw." Cooper's voice was almost pleasant. "So we've finally found something we can agree on, Ken."

"Nobody's going to hit anybody." Sarah held out a restraining hand. "This isn't the way I'd have chosen to tell you, Cooper. But I haven't been sure myself what I was going to do. Not until tonight. And now that I *am* sure…" She looked up at Ken as if she was pleading, and then back at Cooper. "Please, darling—wish me happy. Because…" She took a deep breath.. "Because I'm going to marry Ken."

Almost automatically, he turned to look at Hannah, to check whether he'd actually heard correctly. But her expression made him question his senses even more, for she didn't look startled; as he watched, she merely pursed her lips a little and nodded.

As if in the distance, he heard Sarah continue, "Just as I intended to do more than thirty-five years ago."

*   *   *

It was absolutely none of Hannah's business. No matter what Sarah chose to do with her life, and no matter how Cooper greeted his mother's decisions, it had nothing to do with Hannah.

And, no matter how much she would like things to be different, it never would be any of her concern.

By the time the bar association's banquet had dragged to a close and they returned to Barron's Court, Hannah had mentally repeated at least a million times that no matter what the Winstons did, she had no right to comment.

The smartest thing for her to do was remain detached. Aloof.

In the elevator, as if he was throwing out a challenge, Cooper said, "You've been suspiciously quiet all evening."

Hannah shrugged, trying to keep the gesture casual. "No more than you have. You obviously had a lot to think about, and I decided that it wouldn't be appropriate for me to voice an opinion on a personal matter."

"I never noticed that stopping you before." His voice was dry. "Business or personal."

The tip of her tongue was beginning to feel sore from being bitten, Hannah realized.

"You believe she's serious, don't you?"

"Well," Hannah said judiciously, "considering the way she laughed when you suggested she was being black-mailed into marriage—"

"And you think I didn't handle the whole thing very well." He obviously wasn't asking a question.

Hannah threw detachment to the winds. If Cooper didn't want her opinion, she decided, then he shouldn't have invited it. But since he had... "She is your mother, after all—not your teenage daughter. She's old enough to make up her own mind. And it's not as if she's taken up with a

Hell's Angel who has tattoos and a nose ring. Ken's a successful and respected member of society. So when you suggested that Sarah should be locked up in a padded cell till she regains her senses... Yes, I think a different approach might have been more productive.''

''I was startled.''

''I managed to guess that.'' She waited as he unlocked the door of the penthouse.

Inside, he turned to stare at her, his face intent. ''You, on the other hand, weren't even surprised.''

''Not totally,'' Hannah admitted.

''Why not? What did you see that I missed?''

It wasn't what I saw exactly, she thought almost sadly, *but my point of view.* One woman in love could apparently spot another one—even if she didn't consciously recognize what she was looking at. Of course, she could hardly explain it to Cooper that way. ''It was the way she insulted him, I think. There was personal pain behind it, not just a matter of a principle he'd violated.''

''Exactly. But if he caused her so much personal pain, I think it's a little strange that she's in such a hurry to marry him.''

''If she doesn't want to wait, why should she? She's waited thirty-five years already.''

''I suppose you think it's romantic—announce the engagement on Saturday night, get married on Monday. And I suppose you wanted to cry over all that hogwash about how Mother was furious with Ken all those years ago because he took on Isobel as a client, so she gave his ring back and married my father on the rebound—''

''What I think doesn't matter.'' Hannah hung her cape in the guest closet. ''But I can understand how it happened. Ken was just starting out and struggling financially. He was trying to prove to her very successful family that he was worthy of her, so he was taking clients wherever he could find them.''

"Including Isobel."

"Why not? That affair surely wasn't the kind of thing the family talked about casually, and if he didn't know how Isobel fit into the picture, how could he guess that Sarah would be so furious that she'd throw him over rather than even talk about it?" Hannah paused. "You don't suppose your grandfather sent Isobel to Ken on purpose, hoping that it would break up the romance?"

Cooper frowned. "The stories I've heard about Irving— yeah, he would have been capable. What I don't see is why Ken didn't just dump Isobel as soon as he knew."

Hannah shook her head. "Once Sarah had broken off the engagement, he didn't think it mattered what he did, because it wouldn't bring her back. He probably thought there was no point in losing a client, too."

"So now they've decided to pretend it never happened. As if they can."

He was right about that, of course. But what Sarah had actually said, Hannah reflected, was not nearly as unrealistic as Cooper's interpretation. His mother had talked instead about seizing the moment. Accepting what was possible. Admitting mistakes and acting to correct them— even if the amends came thirty-five years late...

In the long years to come, Hannah wondered, would she—like Sarah—come to regret the decision she had made? Would she lament the fact that she had turned her back on the joy she could have shared with Cooper, simply because she couldn't have everything she wanted? Had she acted too quickly?

Perhaps, she admitted. If she could turn back the clock and make a different decision...

She stole a glance at Cooper. Did he even want her anymore?

She swallowed tears and tried to keep her voice light. "And just think, Cooper—once Ken and Sarah are married, Kitty won't just be your neighbor, she'll be your stepsister. You lucky guy, having her running in and out all the time—"

Cooper caught her arm, swung her around to face him, and growled, "Don't you dare threaten me like that!"

Hannah looked up into his eyes and watched in awe as the playful light which had momentarily gleamed there faded and died away as he looked at her. "Dammit," he said hoarsely. "I can't even look at you without wanting to take you to bed."

Hannah passed the tip of her tongue over her dry lips and said, very softly, "Then why don't you?"

For the space of a heartbeat, her world hung in the balance.

The pressure of his fingers on her arm eased. *I called his bluff,* Hannah thought miserably, *and now he's pulling away.* She closed her eyes so she wouldn't see rejection in his face, and ducked her head so he couldn't see the hurt in hers.

He cupped her chin in his hand, and suddenly his mouth was against hers, hot and fierce and intense. Hannah's knees buckled, and he easily took her weight against him, molding her into his body, making every nerve in her body sizzle. "One more kiss like that," he said unsteadily, "and it will be too late to change your mind."

She had trouble finding her voice. "You really think it would take another one to make it too late?"

He forced her chin up. "This is serious, Hannah. If you're going to regret this in the morning, you'd better tell me now."

"I'd say that depends entirely on you," she murmured. "*Will* I regret it?"

Laughter flared in his eyes. "Not a chance, honey," he whispered. "I'll make sure of it." His touch seemed to melt through the silk of her dress to set her skin aflame.

The combination of passion and humor in him reminded her of what an enormous error it would be to let him guess that this instant was so much more significant to her than it could possibly be to him. And so she ruthlessly squashed the desire to beg him to care about her. She locked in her heart the secret knowledge of her love for him, and she reached instead for what they could share—and discovered with him a joy which stunned her with its shattering beauty.

She slept, curled around him, and she didn't know how much later it was when the chill of being alone in his big bed roused her.

When she sat up, she saw him standing at the window, looking out over the quiet glow of the city to where the first faint light of dawn peeked over the horizon.

"So you're the one who's having regrets." Her voice was low and passion-roughened.

He shook his head, but he didn't turn around. "Just thinking about Mother."

Hannah had no trouble interpreting that statement. He was debating important issues...and Hannah herself wasn't one of them.

Why the surprise? she asked herself. *You knew this was only a moment snipped from time.*

"I don't know what to do about her, Hannah."

She pushed the pillows around, then reconsidered and slid out of bed, reaching for the starched shirt he'd dropped on the floor. In a pinch, it would do as a robe. "That's simple," she said crisply. "First, you tell her you're sorry for the way you greeted her news. Second, you act like a good sport and shake hands with Ken. And then all you have to do is figure out what to buy them for a wedding gift.''

He came across the room to her. ''You make it all sound so easy.'' Slowly, he pushed the shirt off her shoulders and traced the delicate lines of her bones with a fingertip.

Hannah shrugged. ''It's pretty clear.''

Very deliberately, he kissed the hollow at the base of her throat, and she gave a little sigh and surrendered to the desire rising once more inside her.

And she thought, *If only everything could be so simple.*

Cooper might struggle over the question of a wedding gift, but there was no doubt in Hannah's mind about what she would give the newlyweds.

The Lovers' Box. It was the perfect choice.

Of course, she admitted, giving the box to Ken and Sarah meant that she couldn't exactly keep her promise to Cooper—but she was certain he wouldn't mind. He'd only wanted the Lovers' Box for his mother's sake in the first place. So what better way was there to return it to the family than as a wedding gift to the couple it had once divided?

On Monday morning Hannah stopped at the bank and retrieved the box from the safe-deposit vault. Tucking it under her arm, she went on to work. From time to time, she looked up from her papers to study the box, sitting innocently on the corner of her desk.

Such a small and simple thing it was. Yet it—and what it represented—had separated Ken and Sarah, and kept them apart for thirty-five years. And it had brought Hannah and Cooper together, for a brief time at least. She wasn't foolish enough to ask for more.

The Lovers' Box still possessed no particular beauty in Hannah's eyes. It was an interesting artifact, but mostly because of the story behind it rather than its intrinsic qualities. Her original assessment, made the first day she'd seen it, had been correct, she concluded. The box's proportions were awkward, the carving was less than professional, and the surface had dulled with age.

She picked up the box and ran her fingertips across the geometric pattern carved into the thick lid. The wood was good quality, and where it wasn't carved, the surface had been sanded to velvet smoothness; at least there was no threat of picking up a splinter by handling it.

But the box could stand some attention, she thought. A little beeswax and some good hard rubbing would shine it up nicely, and then the Lovers' Box would be ready—just in time for the wedding ceremony to be held at the penthouse that evening. She couldn't wait to see Sarah's face when she opened the package.

And Cooper's, as well. What would he think, when he realized that—in a sense—Hannah was keeping her end of the bargain early? Would her expression of trust make a difference to him?

Don't get your hopes up, Hannah warned herself.

She gave a last stroke to the top of the box and started to set it back on her desk, but it slipped out of her hands. She grabbed frantically for it, trying to banish nightmarish twin pictures—the box lying broken at her feet, and her attempting to explain to Cooper that the damage had been a recent accident, not the result of a temper tantrum on the very day the box had come into her possession. For an instant, she even wished she hadn't been so stubborn about letting him inspect the box. If she'd only taken him to the bank as he'd requested—

She caught the box barely an inch from the floor, snagging it with her fingernails. The only thing which actually stopped its fall was the fact that she'd jammed one nail under the brass knob on the front of the box's lid. Glad that the box had avoided disaster, but still wanting to swear over the damage to her manicure, Hannah tried to extricate the nail without breaking it or scraping off the polish.

Pressing on the knob would release the catch and open the box, but that would only increase the pressure on her fingernail. However, if she could ease the knob out a fraction instead…

As she pulled, the knob moved, and abruptly her fingernail was free.

Annoyed at the sight of the damage, Hannah frowned at the ragged tear across the top of the nail. She set the box down so she could reach for an emery board, and she was filing the tear when she realized that there was something wrong with the top of the Lovers' Box.

It must have twisted as it fell, she thought, breaking the old glue, because one of the joints in the lid had opened up. Instead of a single piece, the top of the box had split into two segments, the carved section and an underlying flat support. Now there was a gap showing between the layers—a small, shallow opening.

Funny, though—it didn't look as if it was broken. Instead, it seemed almost as if the hollow was intended to be there. And indeed, on closer inspection she saw that tucked down inside the empty space was something which appeared to be a folded sheet of paper.

So, she thought, the Lovers' Box wasn't empty after all. And she hadn't broken it, just discovered the secret compartment it had concealed.

But what could be hiding inside?

CHAPTER NINE

HER letter opener was too thick, the long ruler too wide. The emery board had the right proportions to slide into the narrow opening in the top of the Lovers' Box, but its rough surface made it difficult to maneuver in the shallow space. Hannah fiddled for several minutes, trying to snag the folded edge of the paper so she could extract it from the hidden compartment.

"As stubborn as it's being," she muttered, "it's probably a love letter from Irving to Isobel." If that was the case, she told herself, it was just a good thing she was the one who'd found it, instead of Sarah.

Finally the emery board caught, and Hannah tugged gently until the paper slid out. As she unfolded it, she realized why the packet had been so difficult to extract; there were two sheets instead of one, and the paper was heavy—almost like parchment. It didn't look old, exactly, but...

Hannah started to laugh at the wild ideas which suddenly began racing through her head. From what Cooper had told her, the box had belonged to a seafaring man—his ancestor, the Captain, who had brought it home from a voyage as a gift for his bride. But it could be even older than that. What if its original owner had been a pirate? Maybe she was holding an ancient treasure map. Or maybe the Captain himself had been a pirate!

Then Hannah saw the printing on the front of the top sheet, and she froze, her fingers curling tight on the paper.

It's not a treasure map, she thought numbly. *But the Lovers' Box is certainly a treasure chest.*

The papers she held were bearer bonds—securities which carried no specific owner's name but which could be claimed by anyone who had possession of them. Perfectly legitimate, though far from the safest or most lucrative of investments, bearer bonds could be used to transfer funds easily from one place to another. More often, though, their anonymous nature allowed the details of a business deal to be kept quiet, or the ownership of property to remain cloudy.

In fact, bearer bonds were just as liquid and almost as untraceable as hard cash. The only major difference, Hannah thought, was that actual currency would take up more space.

In this case, *far* more space...because the total value of the two bonds she was holding so tightly—the two sheets of paper that she had expected to be nothing more than a long-lost love letter—was just a little more than a million dollars.

Once she stopped shaking, it didn't take long for Hannah to figure out the secret of the Lovers' Box. When she pressed on the brass knob, the catch released to open the main compartment. But when she pulled hard on the knob, as she had done almost accidentally when she'd tried to free her fingernail, the secret compartment in the lid popped open.

It was not a terribly cunning mechanism; she'd seen Chinese puzzle boxes which were far more intricate. But who would think to fiddle with the tarnished knob on an old carved box which wasn't even good enough quality to be considered art? Who would expect such a trinket to contain anything of value—much less a fortune?

Which led Hannah to a question she didn't want to ask. Who else knew the secret of the Lovers' Box?

Sarah probably knew—for there wouldn't be much point in having a family heirloom with a hidden compartment if the family didn't know the secret.

Had Sarah passed on the knowledge to Cooper? There wasn't any reason for her to do so, Hannah concluded, because the box had been gone from the family before he'd even been born.

Had Isobel known? Probably, for Irving, when he gave her the box, would no doubt have showed her its secrets. Besides, it seemed most likely to Hannah that it had been Isobel who had put the bonds in the box. They didn't appear to be old enough to have been stored away by Irving—though Hannah had to admit that she didn't know exactly when he'd died.

At any rate, Isobel had had possession of the Lovers' Box for thirty-five years; who else—apart from Irving, of course—would have had easy access to it in that time?

And perhaps more to the point—even if Isobel didn't know the secret, why would anyone else be foolish enough to store such a liquid asset in a place that Isobel controlled? A place where she might stumble across it at any time, just as Hannah had accidentally done?

Besides, stashing a million dollars' worth of bonds where only she knew where to find them sounded exactly like Isobel. Living up to the last dollar of her income, leaving herself with no security and nothing to fall back on, did not.

Hannah had always been dissatisfied with the idea that Isobel had died without a penny to her name—not because she coveted the money herself, but because it seemed so unlike the old lady she had known. It was much more reasonable to think that Isobel's cunning would have led her to protect herself by tucking away a sizable nest egg.

What didn't make any sense was that she had left the whole works to Hannah while failing to give her any more than a hint about the value of the Lovers' Box.

Perhaps she'd forgotten about the bonds? Not likely, Hannah thought. Isobel wasn't the sort to mislay a million dollars.

Hannah chewed on a pencil and tried to remember exactly what Isobel's will had said about the Lovers' Box. *It is the thing I treasure most,* something like that. And then, *I hope that for my sake Hannah will take good care of it.* But the sentimental comments had been all the instructions Hannah had received.

"For all she knew," Hannah muttered, "I might have ignored her soppy request and done as Cooper feared I would—tossed it in the nearest garbage can!"

As Cooper feared I would.

At the time, she'd found it charming that he was so unusually nostalgic, afraid that she would destroy the family icon which meant so much to his mother.

While in fact...

Hannah's stomach lurched. How easy it had been to convince herself just minutes ago that Cooper didn't know the secret of the Lovers' Box. But of course he did. The secret hiding place was part of the legend of the Lovers' Box, right along with the stories of how it had come into the family and how it had been manipulated away. Sarah would have told him every detail.

Cooper might not have known, as he sat in Ken's office that day, precisely what was inside the secret compartment, but Hannah was absolutely certain he had known there was a secret space. And the fact that Isobel had singled the

Lovers' Box out in her will must have told him it was worth pursuing.

Another memory flitted through Hannah's mind. Cooper, sitting in Ken Stephens's office, saying almost hoarsely, "So what did Isobel say about the box?"

He'd wanted to know if she'd given away the secret, Hannah thought. If, in fact, Isobel had left any hint at all. And when he'd realized that she hadn't, he'd made his move and offered Hannah five hundred dollars in exchange for the box.

A pittance indeed. Not even enough to be a respectable finder's fee.

And ever since that day, he'd been trying to get the Lovers' Box away from her. Not because of its sentimental value or because of the family legend, as he'd claimed, but because he knew—or at least suspected—that it contained something well worth going after.

It appeared to Hannah that when dealing with her had seemed to take too long, Cooper had turned to romancing her. And when that hadn't gotten him anywhere, either, he'd issued a challenge for her to show the Lovers' Box to him, to prove that she hadn't harmed it.

She wondered what he would have done if she had actually swallowed the bait and taken him to the bank. Tried to distract her so he could sneak a look? Maybe even attempted a sleight-of-hand trick to swap the real box for an imitation?

But that gambit, too, had failed, and so he'd gone back to romancing—with a great deal more success the second time around. In the last two days, he'd made love to her as if she was the most precious thing in the universe. But every whisper, every kiss, every caress now appeared to have been a lie. A calculated move in a campaign to make her believe that he cared about her, so that ultimately he could more easily manipulate her into giving the box back.

Hannah felt sick.

Cooper whistled softly, enjoying his upbeat mood, as he wended through the rows of cubicles on his way to find Hannah.

Though he still believed his mother's hasty wedding was an ill-advised affair, he'd said his piece and now he could do no more.

And—speaking of affairs, he thought with a grin—there was Hannah. That entire matter, in his considered opinion, was going very well indeed.

Her back was turned, and she was concentrating so intently on the computer screen that she didn't seem to hear him, so he leaned against the wall of her cubicle and watched her for a moment.

She'd been enticing enough when he'd only been able to imagine what lay under those tailored suits; now that he had firsthand knowledge, she was even more so.

He moved across the cubicle and leaned over her, intending to kiss the nape of her neck. She straightened so abruptly that she almost collided with his chin, and as she turned her chair toward him, her lips brushed the corner of his mouth.

"That's good," Cooper murmured. "I always did like a woman who knew what she wanted and didn't hesitate to go after it." He leaned a little closer.

Inexplicably, Hannah had moved, and his lips touched only air.

"You're obviously feeling good," she said.

Cooper didn't miss a beat. "Not as good as I could feel. If we hurry home—"

She turned back toward her computer. "Sorry. I still have a lot to do."

"The wedding's in two hours."

"I know—it's the wedding I have to get ready for."

"If you're talking about getting dressed, it shouldn't take two hours. And everything else for the wedding should be all taken care of." He grinned. "Even I have to admit there's one good thing about marrying in haste—there's no fussing about the details."

She didn't join in the humor. "I have to shop for a really good beeswax furniture polish and some brass cleaner."

"For what? I'm sure Mrs. Abbott has the place spotless by now."

Hannah shook her head. "Not to clean the penthouse. It's for the Lovers' Box."

Cooper felt a chill creep over him as if a dark cloud had suddenly blocked the sun. "What about the Lovers' Box?"

Her eyes didn't quite meet his. "Didn't I mention my idea to you? I'm going to give it to Sarah and Ken for their wedding."

His ears were buzzing, and his tongue felt thick. "You're...what?"

"It seems only fitting, don't you think? But it could use a little polishing first. For as big a deal as she made out of having it, Isobel didn't seem to pay much attention to the poor thing. The knobs and hinges are discolored, and the wood is dry."

"I don't think that's a good idea."

"Cleaning it, or giving it to Sarah and Ken?" She didn't give him a chance to answer. "I think it's the perfect gift. If they'd had the box last time around they'd have been together for thirty-five years by now."

"So now you believe in that superstition?"

"Not exactly. Let's just say that if Isobel hadn't had the box, and hadn't gone looking for an attorney, Ken and Sarah would have been together." She paused before adding dryly, "I realize you might feel a little hesitation about that, Cooper, since your whole existence hinges on the fact that they *didn't* get married, but I still think it's the least I can do for them."

He took a deep breath. "But we made a deal, Hannah."

"Yes," she admitted. "But you only agreed to it because you wanted the box to give to your mother. That's what you told me. Right?"

The question was clear and direct, and it had only one possible answer. Cooper wanted to swear. "Yes, but—"

"I'm just cutting out the middleman, as it were. In another week or two I'll have found a job and we'd have everything settled anyway, so why should Sarah wait any longer to have the box back? At least I'm assuming I can trust you to play your part for another week or two?" Hannah gave him a dismissive smile. "I'll never get done if we keep talking. Look, I'll be there as soon as I can, Cooper."

There was nothing left for him to do but to silently turn on his heel. He didn't whistle as he walked back through the cubicles; he was too busy thinking.

He needed a new plan, and fast—because suddenly his time was running out.

With a generous application of polish and a firm rubdown, the Lovers' Box looked quite appealing, Hannah thought. And very, very innocent.

She was just nesting it in tissue paper inside a decorative carton when she heard Abbott ushering Sarah and Ken into the living room. She put the lid on, added a bow, and with the carton under her arm she hurried out to greet them.

Sarah kissed her warmly on the cheek; Ken, to Hannah's surprise, did the same. She set her package on the coffee table. "Cooper will be along any minute, I'm sure."

"I'm glad he's not here just yet," Ken said. "We owe you a big thanks, Hannah, for intervening with Cooper as you did so he gave up his opposition to our being married."

"Everything I said was just common sense," Hannah said uncomfortably. In an effort to change the subject, she pushed the package toward them. "I'd like you to open this one now."

Sarah raised an eyebrow. "Before things get crazy?"

"Before there are lots of people around—in case you don't want to explain."

Sarah lifted the lid off the carton and reached in. When she pulled out the Lovers' Box, she sat and looked at it for a full minute without saying a word. Hannah held her breath, until she saw tears brim in Sarah's eyes.

"I had no idea you realized how much this means to me," Sarah whispered.

Guilt tugged at Hannah's heart. *Because if I understood I should have given it back right away,* she thought, *instead of holding it over Cooper's head—and Sarah's.*

Ken sounded almost hoarse. "This is…very thoughtful of you, Hannah."

"And very unlike Isobel?" Hannah said wryly.

"I wouldn't go that far," Ken said. "She wasn't quite the scheming harridan that many people thought she was."

Cooper among them, Hannah thought. And perhaps he'd had reason; if Isobel had seen through him and realized his real motives for wanting to buy the Lovers' Box, she might have acted like the harridan he thought her…

But that made no sense, Hannah realized. He'd tried to buy the box from Isobel—but only an idiot would have sold it to him without removing her treasure first. He had to know that.

Or did he believe that the box contained something of Irving's? Something that Isobel might not even know about? If that was the case, the hints in Isobel's will had no doubt set him straight.

Which left one question still nagging at Hannah. Why had Isobel given only hints of the box's contents—hints which Hannah found vague and meaningless but which Cooper had no trouble interpreting?

It seemed almost as if Isobel had *wanted* Cooper to end up with the Lovers' Box and its contents. But if she didn't want Hannah to have the hidden bonds, why had Isobel dragged her into it at all? Why hadn't she simply left the box to Cooper?

Was it pride that had made her arrange things so indirectly instead?

Almost on a whim, Hannah asked, "Did Isobel leave anything else, Ken? I don't mean material things. But was there any kind of message or letter? Anything more than what she said in the will?"

A look of incredulity crossed Ken's face. "As a matter of fact," he said slowly, "there's a letter for you."

That explains it, Hannah thought with relief. *She might have expected me to recognize a hint when I heard one, but she wasn't unrealistic enough to expect me to interpret it without help.*

"It's sealed, of course," he went on, "and she never told me what was in it."

That figured, Hannah thought. If Ken had known there was a million dollars at stake, he wouldn't have forgotten. She tried to keep her voice level. "And I suppose the letter had slipped your mind entirely till I jolted your memory just now?"

"Of course not. She made arrangements for you to receive it six months to the day after she died."

Hannah frowned. Why a six-month delay? By then the Lovers' Box could have been sold, destroyed, stolen... For a crafty old lady, Isobel had made a lot of very strange arrangements. "I have to wait six months to find out what's in the letter?"

"No. She said you could have it earlier, but only if you specifically requested it." Ken grinned. "That's why I must have looked horn-swoggled when you asked. I thought Isobel was a little off kilter, because she seemed to think that you'd take a while to consider things, but you'd end up reading her mind. The lady sure had you figured out, didn't she?"

Hannah half expected Sarah to challenge the admiring note in his voice, but the older woman didn't seem to notice. She was holding the Lovers' Box as gently as if it were made of bubbles. Hannah wondered if she was restraining herself from giving the knob a pull, just to see if there might be something inside.

"I'm not sure it's such a good thing to know that Isobel and I seem to think alike," Hannah said dryly.

"The letter is in the safe in my office." Ken frowned. "I'm trying to think who has the combination and will be there tomorrow."

"No hurry. I'll get it in a few days, when your honeymoon is over." *Now that I know what it must say,* Hannah thought, *it hardly matters when I read it.*

Ken reached for Sarah's hand. "Now that's another question entirely, because I don't expect the honeymoon ever will be over."

His bride-to-be gave him a misty smile.

Cooper came in, rubbing his hands together. "Sorry,"

he said as he kissed his mother. "I didn't expect to get held up by a telephone call. Is the judge here yet?"

Hannah noted the precise instant that he saw the Lovers' Box resting in his mother's lap, and for a moment she thought he was simply going to seize it. But he maintained his self-control; only a twitching muscle at the corner of his mouth and the cool, almost accusing look in his eyes hinted at his annoyance.

The doorbell rang.

"That must be the judge now," Cooper said. "I suppose we should clear up some of this mess so we aren't tripping over loose papers during the ceremony."

There was no doubt in Hannah's mind about which part of the mess he intended to take charge of. She moved as quickly as she could to forestall him. "Sarah, if you'll let me put that back in its carton—"

Just as she took hold of the Lovers' Box, Abbott ushered Kitty into the room.

"I'll help," Cooper said.

"Nonsense," Hannah said just as firmly. "You've hardly had a chance to say hello, so just relax—I'll get things out of sight."

Kitty released a trill of laughter. "Oh, do let Hannah take care of it, Cooper," she said. "She has nothing better to do. But if you and I are going to stand up with the bride and groom, there are things we need to rehearse."

"I don't see any need to practice handing over a ring."

Kitty had wrapped both hands around his arm. "But we want it all to go smoothly, don't we?" She tugged. "And we only have a few minutes."

Cooper looked over his shoulder. "I think Mrs. Abbott has been putting the other gifts in the library as they arrive."

"What a good idea," Hannah said. "It'll be a nice, private place to look at them later."

Was it her imagination, or did Cooper's eyes narrow speculatively before he turned his attention to Kitty?

"While I'm thinking of it, Hannah," Ken said, "there's something else we'll need to talk about when Sarah and I get home."

Hannah paused with her hands buried in tissue paper, wondering what he could mean. He had no idea she was planning to resign, so it couldn't be that. Had Brenton come up with another scheme to discredit her?

"The foundation needs better legal representation," Sarah said. "When I asked Ken for his advice, he suggested that you'd be the perfect solution—since you have ties to both the foundation, through Cooper, and the firm."

Not for long, Hannah thought. *And neither one of those relationships can end soon enough to satisfy me!*

She searched instead for a more tactful answer. "I hardly think that I'm experienced enough to take on such a big—"

"Not to handle the whole job, no," Ken said. "That seems to be part of the problem, actually—no one person can handle the entire variety of legal issues the foundation faces, so Sarah's ended up using a sort of patchwork."

"And sometimes things are overlooked," Sarah added.

"You would be acting as a liaison between the foundation and the firm," Ken said, "making sure not only that every legal question is covered, but that it's handled by the most talented people we've got."

It sounded, Hannah had to admit, like a dream job—if only it were possible for her to take it.

"You think it over," Ken said, "and we'll talk about it at the end of the week, as soon as we get home."

Sarah added softly, "I'd feel so much more comfortable

if I could delegate all the legal issues to one person, Hannah—especially when it's a person who not only understands the law but knows how important the foundation is to Cooper and to me.''

It was a good thing no one expected an answer right then, Hannah thought, because her throat was so dry she couldn't have said a word if her life had depended on it.

The wedding ceremony was beautiful, if brief; it was hardly any time before the rings were duly handed over, Ken kissed his brand-new wife, and Kitty—careful not to smudge her mascara—blotted away two of the fakest-looking tears Hannah had ever seen.

Within minutes, guests began arriving for the reception. Hannah stayed on the fringes, glad that this was in no respect her celebration. With Ken and Sarah greeting each arrival, Mrs. Abbott supervising the caterer, and Kitty acting as the focal point and life of the party, nobody was paying any attention to Hannah. Which was fine with her, because she had her own agenda—to keep an eye on Cooper so subtly that he didn't realize he was being watched.

Keeping him at the edge of her peripheral vision had seemed a simple enough idea, but it had been easier to plan than it was to carry out. She lost track of him more than once and had to scan the rooms in order to find him once more. Each time, he was doing something completely innocent—talking to a foundation donor, getting a fresh drink at the bar—and he was nowhere near the library.

She was starting to think she'd been mistaken in believing that he would seize the first opportunity to check out the Lovers' Box.

And if she'd been mistaken about that, was it possible she'd been wrong about other things, as well—like his motives in making love to her?

Dreamer, she accused herself.

She was paying so little attention to anything except Cooper that she nearly walked into Kitty and Brenton having a cozy little twosome in an out-of-the-way corner. She almost apologized before she realized that there was no need because neither of them had seen her. Brenton had his back turned to the room, and Kitty wasn't looking at anything at all; she had her eyes closed while Brenton kissed her.

Hannah was a bit surprised that someone who was so expert at avoiding commitment would make such a public display of his affections. Of course, courting Ken Stephens's daughter was altogether different from stringing along a woman who might or might not turn out to be an heiress...

It was almost amusing to think of how Brenton would have salivated over the pair of bearer bonds she'd found in the Lovers' Box. Almost.

Brenton lifted his head and laughed triumphantly. "How about it, Kitty? Shall we tell them right now?"

"Tell them what?"

"That you're going to marry me, silly."

Kitty's big blue eyes opened wide. "But I'm not."

"This is no time to joke, Kitty. There are weddings in the air—let's take advantage of it."

Kitty stepped away from him. "I'd say it's me you're trying to take advantage of, Brenton."

Hannah watched in utter fascination as Brenton began to sputter. "But...but you said last night—"

Kitty laughed. "You thought because I slept with you I was serious?"

Hannah jumped at the sound of a soft sigh beside her. Sarah muttered, "I've got my work cut out with that girl."

"It's too late," Hannah said under her breath.

Kitty had gone straight on. "You've been mildly entertaining, Brenton, but that's all. The idea that you could get me to fall so far in love with you that I'd do something stupid like asking Daddy to make you a full partner—"

Brenton's face was so red that Hannah wouldn't have been surprised if he'd had a stroke on the spot.

Kitty shook her head. "It was fun to lead you on. But now—oh, do stop bothering me and just go away, Brenton."

"On the other hand," Hannah said softly, "giving Brenton the boot means she has better taste than I gave her credit for."

Sarah choked. "It's not kind of you to make me laugh at a man who's in pain, Hannah—even if he deserves it." But her eyes were sparkling.

Hannah bit back a smile herself. Then she remembered her mission and cast a look around the party.

Cooper was gone.

As unobtrusively as possible, she slipped through the crowd and down the hall to the library. Very quietly, she opened the door.

Cooper was standing at the desk, with his back to the door. In the center of the blotter, where just a couple of hours ago she had carefully placed it, stood the Lovers' Box.

And as Hannah watched, he spread one big hand over the top of the box to hold it steady, and with the other hand tugged on the newly polished brass knob.

With a tiny squeak, the hidden compartment popped open. He bent to look inside, then reached eagerly for the thin-bladed paper knife that Hannah had thoughtfully put within easy reach.

She watched as he extracted a bit of paper, and she recognized disappointment in the lines of his body when he saw that he held not an item of value, but an old photograph of his grandfather.

"What's the matter?" she said softly. "Wasn't that what you expected to find?"

Slowly, Cooper turned toward her, his face filled with guilt.

The last fragment of hope that Hannah had cherished crumbled into ash, leaving behind only a grim sort of satisfaction at being proved right.

With that, she would have to be content. Even if it meant her heart was breaking.

CHAPTER TEN

COOPER'S voice was hoarse. "Hannah—"

She moved a little closer to the desk, letting the door of the library slowly close behind her. "What did you think would be in there, Cooper?"

He took a deep breath. "Not what I actually found, that's for sure."

"Don't bother to mince words. You thought you'd find whatever Isobel had managed to squirrel away. Whatever was left of the money she extorted from your grandfather."

His jaw tightened. "As a matter of fact, that's precisely what I expected."

Hannah reached under her jacket, into the small pocket at the back of her skirt, and pulled out two folded pieces of paper. "Guess what—that's exactly what was in there. Isobel's loot. Not the picture. I put that in because I thought you'd be terribly disappointed to find the hidden compartment completely empty."

Cooper sat down on the corner of the desk. He was still dangling Irving's photograph, with the corner barely held between two fingers. "Now I remember. You found this down in the condo. I wonder if you picked it up because you had this trick planned even then."

A quiver slid up her spine. Why did he suddenly sound relaxed, as if much of the tension had drained out of him? *It's just part of the game to him,* she thought.

"How did you happen to discover the secret, anyway?" Cooper asked. "And when?"

"You're wondering how long I've been holding out on you. Not that it matters. Isobel left the box to me—and that means whatever is inside the box is mine, too. There is no room for disagreement on that point, so you may as well not waste time arguing."

"Oh, I know better than to argue with you," he said dryly. "Last time you were so sure of yourself it cost me fifteen million dollars. How much is involved this time?"

"Not nearly as much." Hannah held up the two sheets of paper. "Bearer bonds. Just a little more than a million dollars' worth, payable to whoever has possession of them." She took two steps toward him and held out the papers, but he didn't take them—so she reached for his hand, folding his fingers around the heavy paper.

She was very proud of herself, for she had neither flinched at touching him nor clung to the warmth of his hand. She'd acted as if he'd been a casual acquaintance, not a lover who had the power to shatter her world.

She was halfway to the door before Cooper spoke, and he sounded as if he'd been hit in the stomach. "What in the hell are you up to now, Hannah?"

She feigned astonishment. "Surely you're not complaining about getting part of your fifteen million back? You shouldn't look a gift horse in the mouth, Cooper. Besides, you're bright. You can figure it out."

"What do you expect me to do with it?"

"Don't you get it? I don't care what you do with it."

"You're handing it over because since Isobel's money came from Irving in the first place, you think it should be returned." He slid off the desk and started toward her. "Hannah—"

Perhaps, she decided, he needed to be slapped with the truth. She paused with her hand on the doorknob. "No. That's not the reason at all. I'm handing the money over because what was hidden in that box—even when you didn't know for certain what it was—was so very important to you. A whole lot more important than…'' *Than I could ever be.* Her voice threatened to break, and she stopped to clear her throat. ''Than anything else.''

She pulled the door open just as Abbott, standing in the hallway, raised his hand to knock.

''Sir—'' he began.

''Dammit, Abbott, not now!'' Cooper reached for Hannah's arm. ''Come back in here—''

''I'm sorry, sir,'' the butler went on, ''but the newlyweds are ready to leave.''

Cooper swore under his breath. ''All right. We're coming.'' He glared at Hannah. ''But don't think we're finished with this. We'll talk later.''

''Sure,'' she said agreeably, and thought, *If it's up to me, it'll be a whole lot later. Like in some future lifetime.*

The answer seemed to satisfy Cooper, for he thrust the bearer bonds into the breast pocket of his jacket—she hadn't expected, of course, that he'd forget about *those*—and turned toward the living room.

With a great deal of hilarity and enough confetti to keep Mrs. Abbott and a cleaning team busy for weeks, Ken and Sarah were off. The rest of the guests trickled away, but just before the last of them left, Hannah tiptoed down the hall to her bedroom, picked up the overnight bag she'd packed as soon as she got home from work that afternoon, and slipped away down the fire stairs to Mrs. Patterson's condo.

Brutus greeted her, tail wagging, and then ran to bring his leash and drop it hopefully at her feet. Mrs. Patterson shooed him away and fixed Hannah a cup of herbal tea.

And Hannah told herself that it was foolish to regret that

she hadn't been able to say a real goodbye to the man she loved.

By ten the next morning, Brenton had sworn at two secretaries, reduced a receptionist to tears, and threatened to fire the attorney in the cubicle next to Hannah's. "I wonder what's eating him today," the attorney muttered through the gap in the cubicle's walls. "Even when he loses a case, he's not usually like this."

"He's been disappointed in love," Hannah said crisply. "Or maybe I should say he's been disappointed in career planning. Where Brenton's concerned, it comes out to just about the same thing." She turned around and saw Brenton standing in the open doorway, glowering at her.

She sighed. It seemed she'd accidentally burned her bridges—but at least it had happened only a bit earlier than she'd planned.

"Before you start chewing on me, Brenton," she announced, "I'd like to tell you that my resignation will be on your desk within fifteen minutes."

"You'd better not be expecting much in the way of a recommendation."

"I don't need one. I've already got a job offer—out of town."

Brenton grinned. "Dumped you, did he? Well, well, well. Don't feel you need to stick around and serve out your notice, Hannah. Frankly, you're not much use around here anymore."

"Oh, I wouldn't leave you in the lurch like that," Hannah said sweetly. "But shall we say two weeks instead of the standard four?"

As soon as he was out of hearing range, she picked up the telephone to call the firm which had offered to hire her, and she was putting the final touches on her formal letter of resignation when the personnel manager broke the news that the job had gone to someone else instead. ''When we didn't hear from you by the end of last week, Ms. Lowe,'' he said sorrowfully, ''we assumed you weren't interested anymore.''

She broke the connection and put her head down in her hands. What an idiot she was, she thought miserably. Once more, she had leaped before looking. And by doing so she'd gotten herself right back where she'd started—Brenton was on the warpath, and she was just about homeless...

Only this time, she had to admit, things were actually worse than before. Now that she'd actually said the words, she couldn't change her mind about resigning; she had no trouble imagining Brenton's sadistic laugh if she were even to broach the subject of staying on.

With the evaporation of the job she'd been offered, and no idea when or where she might find another, she had to have a place to live in the meantime. It was one thing to accept Mrs. Patterson's hospitality for a few days, but if she wasn't going to be leaving the city soon for the new job, she couldn't take advantage of the woman.

And then there was the recommendation she'd so blithely told Brenton she didn't need. If, after all, she went back to him to ask for it...

Whether she did or not, the next two weeks—till she was officially finished at Stephens & Webster—were going to be hellish. In fact, Hannah thought bitterly, she'd rather serve the time in jail than working under Brenton's supervision. Without Cooper to serve as a buffer...

The mere thought of his name sent a wave of pain surging through her. Not that she'd been able to forget him altogether in the meantime, of course; she'd only succeeded in pushing the memory aside, not crushing it—and suddenly it all came flooding back, threatening to submerge her.

It made no sense at all, considering how he'd treated her. But less than twelve hours after she'd walked out of the penthouse, her heart—at least what was left of it—was aching to see him once more.

The Lovers' Box, his duplicity in trying to get control of it, his guilt when she'd caught him red-handed—none of that seemed to matter anymore when compared to the pain of losing him.

Hannah sighed. She'd apparently learned nothing at all.

She almost ran into Cooper that night as she and Brutus returned from a late-evening walk. Fortunately, she'd spotted him half a block away, and by turning up the alley behind Barron's Court—thus giving the pug an unexpected taste of the underside of city life—she avoided the encounter.

The next day, she closed the elevator door almost in Cooper's face. Later she dodged him at the front entrance of Barron's Court by climbing into a cab she neither wanted nor could afford.

Each near-encounter left her aching for what they had shared. Or, more accurately, what she had thought they shared. *It isn't really the same thing at all.*

On the morning when she finally finished the tedious process of going through the musty boxes of Jacob Jones's papers and gave Brenton her conclusions, he grunted and told her to start over. "It's obvious that in your carelessness you missed something," he said.

She held on to her temper and said mildly, "There was nothing to find, Brenton. There is no magic receipt here that will make the Internal Revenue people excuse Jacob Jones's little error on his tax return."

"Maybe you were just more interested in other things. But now that you're not distracted by your extra activities, I'm sure you'll do a better job this time through."

Hannah's self-control slipped a little. "I can't discover something that isn't there. Face it, Brenton, your client is a crook. Either you already know that, or he's been stringing you on, along with everyone else."

Brenton went on coolly, "And just to be certain that you don't skimp on the job this time, I want a written summary of every single document in those boxes."

"I've got other work to do, Brenton. And I'm only going to be here for ten more days."

"Then you'd better toil like fury, hadn't you?" He dug a hand into the top box and with a malignant smile scattered a stack of papers over her desk. "Here, I'll help you get started."

From the doorway, a calm voice spoke. "What do you mean, Hannah, that you'll only be here for ten more days?" Ken Stephens moved into the cubicle, blocking Brenton's path.

Hannah hadn't seen him come in, and she was certain Brenton hadn't, either. She said as calmly as she could, "I mean that while you were gone, I turned in my resignation."

Ken picked up a crumpled receipt, sniffed the air, and put it down again. "Unpleasant," he said. "But this sort of work needs doing sometimes."

A crafty look came into Brenton's eyes. "That's exactly what I was telling her, Mr. Stephens, but she doesn't seem to want to follow rules."

"I heard what you were telling her." Ken's voice was mild. "You know, Bannister, I've never put much faith in my daughter's skills at character assessment—until you came along. I'll see you in my office in half an hour. And bring Hannah's resignation letter with you.''

''But I don't have it,'' Brenton protested. ''It's already going through the proper channels.''

Ken's eyes narrowed. ''Then chase it, find it, and remove it from the proper channels.''

Brenton seemed to shrink. He sidestepped Ken and hurried away.

''Thanks, Ken,'' Hannah said. ''And welcome home. Is it appropriate to ask if the honeymoon was fun?''

Ken grinned, but he didn't answer. ''I brought Isobel's letter down for you.'' He handed over a pale blue envelope, so thin it could contain nothing more than a single sheet of paper. ''Have you had a chance to look over the foundation materials I had sent down to you?''

''A little, but there hasn't been much time. Brenton has had other priorities for me.''

''Don't let Brenton disturb you anymore. He's not going to be here much longer.''

Hannah bit her lip. ''I hope you won't make any hasty decisions about him.''

Ken's eyebrows rose. ''Are you defending Mr. Bannister?''

''No. If it was up to me, I'd have him tarred and feathered. But there are rules about getting rid of employees, and I'd hate it if an effort to protect me backfired on you, Ken. I don't know how much you heard, but—''

''Quite enough. Putting it together with Kitty's observations and what Cooper told me about the reasons behind your…uh, romance…''

She looked down at her hands, clasped on the edge of her desk. Some explanation had been necessary, she supposed, about why she was no longer living in the penthouse. But why Cooper couldn't have just glossed the sit-

uation over... Because he didn't want to take any more of
the blame than he had to, she supposed. And making her
look bad would allow him to appear less of a villain.

"You'll withdraw your resignation, of course, Hannah."

She closed her eyes and pictured a professional future
brighter than she'd dared to dream of. No Brenton to deal
with. A new position as liaison with the foundation. The
chance to work with clients like Sarah instead of ones like
Jacob Jones...

But working with Sarah and the foundation—or even
doing something as simple as socializing with her boss—
would mean running into Cooper.

After what he had done, could she bear to encounter
him, greet him politely, treat him like any other person?
Could she keep her anger from getting in the way?

And perhaps more important, even if she could control
her anger, what about her love?

Her feelings hadn't changed just because she had
abruptly discovered that Cooper wasn't worthy of them.
Only time would dissipate the pain of loving him.

Lots of time. And maybe lots of distance.

She sighed. "I just don't know right now, Ken."

After he was gone, Hannah sat for a long time staring
into space, and finally she opened Isobel's letter.

The handwriting was firm and strong, and the words
were just as no-nonsense; as she read the letter, Hannah
could almost hear Isobel speaking.

"By the time you read this," the letter began, "I've
either been gone for six months or you've figured out that
something was missing and asked Ken Stephens for an
explanation. I don't know which, but I hope it's the latter,
Hannah. I'd like to think you're perceptive enough not
only to suspect what I've done but to figure out why."

Because you wanted to help me evade the inheritance

tax, Hannah thought. *Bearer bonds—how obvious can you be?*

"In a word," the letter went on, "Brenton. He's quite charming and delightful, isn't he? An unselfish mentor, a thoughtful boss, a warm and affectionate man."

So much for Isobel's judgment.

"That's why I constructed my will as I did—in the hope that when he finds out you're not an heiress after all, Brenton won't be able to keep his true nature—sadistic, perverted, and calculating—from showing."

Hannah released a low whistle. *Sorry, Isobel, for thinking he'd fooled you.*

In fact, she realized, the cunning old lady had double-crossed him—making Brenton think she'd fallen for his charm, encouraging him to believe that Hannah would inherit a fortune, so he'd be even more likely to blow up when his hopes were smashed....

"At any rate," Isobel went on, "by now you should have had plenty of time to see him as he is and disentangle yourself. If you haven't done so, you deserve the treatment you'll get from him. But I'm betting you're wiser than that—and it was never my intention to leave you with nothing, only to discourage you from letting Brenton share it."

Hannah skipped over the instructions for opening the hidden compartment in the Lovers' Box and went on to the next paragraph, where the tartness returned to Isobel's words.

"If you've thrown the box away in a fit of pique at me for leaving you something so worthless," the letter said, "then you didn't deserve to have what's inside. If you've sold it to Cooper Winston for a small fortune in an attempt to buy back Brenton's affections, then you also don't deserve the contents. On the other hand, if you've let Cooper

charm you out of the Lovers' Box, I completely understand, and I hope you enjoy him as much as I enjoyed—''
The handwriting broke off, and then took up again in a
stronger, larger style. ''Well, there are topics which
shouldn't be committed to paper, even by those who are
soon to be dead and gone. So I'll just say, some things are
more important than money, and if you've found them
with Cooper, then you're a lucky woman.''

The mist in Hannah's eyes made the signature look
blurry.

A lucky woman.

If only Isobel had been right.

Hannah and Brutus had gone all the way from Barron's
Court up Grand Avenue to the governor's mansion and
back, and by the time they reached the lobby again the
pug was breathing hard.

The elevator was standing open. Hannah hurried the dog
across the lobby, pushed the button for the fifth floor, and
bent to release Brutus's leash from his collar. ''How many
times have I told you that if you didn't pull so hard you
wouldn't be out of breath when—''

Just as the elevator doors began to close, the dog yipped
and darted out into the lobby once more. Hannah, caught
with his leash dangling, was stunned; Brutus had never
done anything of the sort before. She jammed her hand
between the doors, forced them open again, and went after
him.

Brutus, yipping almost hysterically, made a beeline for
a man standing in the center of the lobby. From six feet
away, he hurled himself at Cooper's knees; Cooper
stooped to catch him and stood up with the pug in his
arms.

Brutus snuffled at Cooper's shirt pocket, then sighed and

settled down, his eyes half closed and his neck stretched out so Cooper could more easily scratch his chin.

"That's disgusting," Hannah muttered. Of course, her conscience reminded, if she had been the one cuddled in Cooper's arms, she might look just as idiotically contented... "Thanks for capturing him. I'll take him off your hands now." She reached out for the dog.

Brutus opened his eyes halfway and growled at her.

Hannah's jaw dropped. "Listen, you stupid animal—"

"Brutus has never bitten you," Cooper pointed out. "And it's funny that you were never so concerned when he was growling at me on a regular basis."

"That was different." She caught herself. "I mean—"

"Never mind explaining. There are more important things to attend to just now. You agreed that we were going to finish our talk—but then you ran away. And you've been very efficiently avoiding me ever since."

"I didn't run. I simply left, because I thought we'd said everything we needed to."

"Wrong—we still have a lot to say. As I see it, because you didn't stick around to discuss it then, you now have three choices. We either take up the discussion right here in the lobby, or you come upstairs with me where Daniel the doorman can't listen in."

"And my third choice?" Hannah asked warily.

He reached into his shirt pocket and held up a dog biscuit. Brutus perked up and barked, and Cooper gave him the treat. "I'll start carrying doggie candy in all my pockets, so anytime I'm within a block Brutus won't just run to me, he'll use his leash to drag you along." His fingers didn't stop their easy caress of the pug's chin. "What's so bad about talking to me, Hannah? Are you afraid I might knock a hole in that self-righteous armor of yours?"

She shrugged. "I don't have anything to say."

"Good. Then you can shut up and listen—because I do have a few things to tell you." With the dog still cradled in one arm, he took her elbow and guided her toward the elevator.

In the penthouse, he put Brutus down—to the pug's dismay—and led Hannah into the library.

She shivered, though the room itself wasn't as chilly as her memories of finding him there with the Lovers' Box open in his hand. "Can't we talk somewhere else?"

"Any unpleasant recollections you have of this room are ones you created."

"Oh, really? I suppose I should have just stayed out of it and let you snoop!"

"I wasn't snooping. I was investigating."

"Right. By that logic, Brutus never really growled at you—he was just whispering sweet nothings."

The pug, hearing his name, looked up hopefully from where he'd flopped on the rug in front of the empty fireplace.

Cooper had gone round the desk and pulled open the top drawer. He took out an envelope and tossed it across to her.

Hannah said, "Oh, did you get a letter from Isobel, too?"

"No, this isn't a letter. She did leave one for you, then? I suspected she had."

"Yes, she did, but that's not how I figured out the secret in the box." The envelope wasn't sealed. She slid a thumbnail under the flap and pulled out an official-looking document. "What's this?"

"Your million dollars. Ken started hyperventilating at the very idea of bearer bonds, so he deposited them in a money-market account in the estate's name. As soon as the paperwork is settled, it'll be turned over to you."

"It's not mine. It was never mine."

"Isobel left it to you."

"Isobel got it from Irving."

"That's beside the point."

"No, that's *precisely* the point. That's why you were going after the Lovers' Box with such intensity—in case there was a chance of getting back what your grandfather had thrown away."

"No."

She waited for more, but the silence dragged until she couldn't stand it any longer. "No, what?"

"That's not why I wanted the Lovers' Box."

"Don't expect me to bite on that sentimental claptrap! You don't believe in the legend, but you certainly had faith in that secret compartment. Oh, I'm sure you'd have lovingly presented the box to your mother—but not till you'd made sure to extract anything of real value. Admit it, Cooper—you were terrified I'd throw a fortune away before you had a chance to get your hands on it."

"You're almost right. I was afraid you'd throw it away, yes—but not because I wanted it. I wanted you to have it."

"Oh, that's funny. You should try a stand-up comedy routine. If that's what you wanted, you could have just said, 'Gee, Hannah, there's a little trick about that box that just might be worth looking into.' But you didn't."

"I should have told you," he agreed.

"You're darned right you should have!"

"I was afraid the box would turn out to be empty, and I didn't want you to be disappointed."

"Your thoughtfulness overwhelms me," Hannah muttered.

"I didn't know what—if anything—Isobel had managed to hang on to. It seemed impossible that she'd spent all of it, because that was a very healthy pension she was drawing. And where would she have been spending it, anyway? She didn't buy anything of value—she either rented it or she found a way to get it free.''

Hannah remembered noticing that very contradiction, but unlike Cooper, she hadn't followed it to the logical conclusion—to wonder where the money had gone instead. She told herself not to feel foolish; that had, after all, been the evening when Brenton first threatened her job, she'd found her bed gone, and she'd made the proposition to Cooper which had culminated in her falling in love with him...

''About the only thing she spent money on was reproducing her jewelry as costume stuff.''

Hannah frowned. ''Reproducing it? What do you mean?''

''It wasn't always fake. But if she was really broke, why didn't she just sell it?''

''Pride,'' Hannah mused.

''Maybe. But I had no evidence, only a gut feeling that she couldn't have thrown that much money away. Still, it wasn't enough to take the chance of raising your expectations.''

''My expectations,'' Hannah said bitterly. ''The same ones you thought were so pretentious and greedy and selfish—''

''At first, yes. Think about how it looked, Hannah. You moved in with an old woman that you were barely related to and who was to all appearances filthy rich, and then you started ingratiating yourself with the whole of Barron's Court by walking dogs, carrying groceries, listening to stories—'' He held up both hands. ''I know, you were only being friendly. I'm just telling you what it looked like.''

"Well, if you were determined to think the worst of me—"

"I was," he admitted. "That was why it took me a while to realize that I was so steamed over Isobel's will not because of the barbs she'd shot at me but because of the way she'd treated you—getting your hopes up and then stomping all over you."

"I never saw it that way," Hannah said. "I didn't expect anything, so I wasn't disappointed. I was just—puzzled."

Cooper nodded. "So was I. I couldn't stop thinking about how much fuss she'd made over the Lovers' Box. She wasn't just crowing over keeping me from having it, she was making sure that everybody knew it was too important to lose track of. But the box itself *wasn't* all that important—to anybody but me—which meant there had to be something in the secret compartment. And that puzzled me even more, because it made no sense for her to tuck something away in the Lovers' Box instead of leaving it to you outright. She had to have a reason for wanting you to have whatever it was eventually—but not right away."

"So that's why you didn't tell me anything about the secret compartment? Because Isobel didn't want me to know?"

He nodded. "Sounds crazy, doesn't it? So I kept quiet and just tried to get my hands on the box so I could take a look."

"Terribly inconvenient of me to tuck it in the bank vault so you couldn't even get close, wasn't it?"

"You can say that again. It was driving me crazy, Hannah. I kept thinking that either I was completely nuts and there was nothing there, or she must have had a darned good reason for doing it that way instead of straight out. It was about then that you popped up again with your crazy proposition, and as soon as I heard about Brenton, I knew what Isobel was up to."

Hannah sighed. "Isobel had some excuse for being worried about what I'd do—but please don't tell me you thought I was idiot enough to want him after he'd made it clear he was only after the money."

"People in love do crazy things, Hannah."

And how could she possibly disagree with that?

"I didn't know you well enough then to judge whether you were telling the truth about your job, or if you were out for revenge, or if you wanted him back."

"Did it matter?"

He took his time answering. "Yes. It mattered."

Her heart fluttered.

But he didn't follow up. Instead, he said, "I finally told myself that whatever was inside the box was perfectly safe, and it wouldn't hurt anyone—you included—to simply leave it there till everybody had a chance to cool off. As soon as you kept your end of the bargain and gave me the box, I'd check it out. Until then, it wasn't going anywhere."

"You looked as if you could strangle me when I told you I was giving it to your mother instead."

"You'd found the bonds by then, hadn't you? You deliberately dangled the box in front of me—"

"I was waiting to see what you'd do. And you did exactly what I expected." Hannah took a deep breath. "This has been a delightful story, Cooper, but you know, there isn't any evidence to support it. You could have made the whole thing up after I caught you—you've had days to tweak every last detail to get it into line. If I hadn't found the secret myself, what's to say you'd have given the bonds to Ken at all? They could have just disappeared into your pocket." She tossed the envelope containing the money-market documents back at him.

"You're right," he said quietly. "There isn't any evidence. And I suppose it was foolish to hope that you'd believe me, without anything to back up my story—if only I could get you to sit still and listen."

There was an odd finality about his voice. Hannah found herself sliding to the edge of her chair as if she'd been dismissed. *But it's not supposed to end like this,* she wanted to say. Instead she swallowed the lump in her throat and fumbled in her pocket for Brutus's leash.

"All I was trying to do," he said quietly, "was to find what was yours—if it existed. How could something which started with such good intentions have gone so wrong?"

If he had argued, she thought suddenly, or added extra details or tried to justify his actions, she would have remained cool and suspicious. But the sadness in his eyes and the slump of his shoulders spoke louder than words.

She had misjudged him. And then she had added to the insult by throwing his honest explanation back in his face. She took a deep breath and tried to figure out how to apologize.

"I suppose it doesn't make an ounce of difference," he said quietly, "that I love you—but unless you believe that, the rest makes no sense whatever."

Hannah's knees were trembling. "You...what?" she said faintly.

Cooper shook his head. "I don't know how it happened, or when. But it wasn't until you came into this room that night and caught me with my fingers in the cookie jar that I realized I'd staked even more on that damned Lovers' Box than I'd realized."

She'd almost forgotten how to breathe.

"At first, I thought it was going to be all right—when

you admitted you'd found the bonds, I was so relieved I was almost giddy.''

Hannah remembered thinking that he'd suddenly and inexplicably relaxed, but it hadn't occurred to her that he might actually be relieved to know that Isobel's treasure not only existed after all, but had gotten safely into the proper hands.

''Then you looked at me as if I was a criminal, and you wouldn't listen when I tried to tell you why I'd done it. And that was when I knew I'd lost a lot more than just an old wooden box. I'd lost everything that mattered to me.''

''You never gave me any sign that I was anything more than a convenience,'' Hannah protested. He looked at her sharply, and she felt herself turn red.

''I told you, Hannah, I didn't know it. I was probably already over the brink when I manipulated you into moving in with me—I've certainly never done anything that crazy before. Maybe it was even before that, clear back when you were setting the dog on me every time we met—'' He'd moved gradually closer.

''I did not!''

On the hearth rug, Brutus gave a single low wuff, as if to say he was insulted by the suggestion.

''Okay,'' Cooper admitted, ''maybe you didn't conspire with the dog.''

''I would have been too scared to do anything of the kind. You were always frowning.''

''Well, of course I was.'' He sounded indignant. ''I couldn't help being attracted to you. That's why I was always so sharp with you. Whatever you did turned me on, and I thought you must know it and be using it deliberately. What was I supposed to do, dance a jig?'' He was close enough that she could feel his breath stirring the hair at her temple, and his fingertips were gentle against her cheek. "Hannah..." His voice was suddenly serious. "Have I lost my mind completely, or are you saying—"

"Am I saying what?" she asked innocently.

"Oh, the hell with it." His hand dropped, and he turned away.

Her fingers closed almost convulsively on his arm.

He swung around and pulled her close. "Gave yourself away, didn't you?"

But there was still hesitation in the way he held her, until she put her arms around his neck and drew him down to her, and whispered, "I love you."

If all of his previous kisses—stunning as they were— had been added together, they couldn't have equaled the impact of this embrace, the first which hid no secrets.

Finally, breathlessly, she said, "All that time, we were being so discreet about our attraction to each other that we didn't even know it ourselves. Remember laughing about that?"

He nodded. His eyes were dark, almost solemn. "Hannah, I swear that I never intended to cheat you. That night when I crept in here to steal a look—"

"Oh, so you're admitting that you're a sneak and a thief!"

"And if you keep that up," he threatened lightly, "I may turn into a wife-beater, too."

Hannah choked.

Cooper frowned. "All right, so I haven't even asked you to marry me yet. But is it that difficult to believe I'm going to?"

"Yes," Hannah said honestly.

"Great. Now that you've said you'll marry me—"

"That wasn't what I was agreeing to!"

He held her a little away from him. "Oh, really?"

She looked into his eyes and drew a deep breath.
"Yes."

"Good." He pulled her down onto his lap, in one of
the big leather chairs by the fireplace; it was just as well,
because by then Hannah wasn't sure she could remember
how to stand up.

Cooper leaned his cheek against her hair. "I never
thought I'd be thanking Isobel for anything. Instead, I'm
thanking her for everything."

"What do you mean? She played a part, of course,
but—"

Cooper shook his head. "No, it was more than that.
Hasn't it occurred to you yet that there was a much safer
and easier way for her to give you those bonds? All she
had to do was tuck them in with the letter she left with
Ken. Instead, she made all that fuss about leaving you the
Lovers' Box and pushing me out in the cold."

Hannah frowned. He was right, she realized. If Isobel
had taken the easy route, then Hannah would have been
sure to end up with the bonds—there would have been no
risk that she might destroy or sell or give away the Lovers'
Box before she found the treasure. And Cooper would
have had what he wanted with no fuss or bother. Hannah
would have had nothing to offer him; Cooper would have
had no need to negotiate...

And they might never have come together.

"She knew how badly I wanted the box," Cooper said.
"But she also knew that I wouldn't submit to being
robbed, because she'd tried that trick herself. Which meant
that any agreement we tried to reach would take a while."

"No," Hannah said unsteadily. "She didn't deliberately
manipulate us into falling in love. She *couldn't.*"

Cooper's voice was cheerful. "I'll go double or nothing
on the bonds that she intended for us to end up like this."

"You can't prove it."

"No. That was always the thing about Isobel—you could never prove anything. But I know it, as sure as I know we're meant to be together." His lips brushed her hair. Hannah turned her face to his and lost herself once more in his kiss.

At their feet, Brutus sat up, his leash in his mouth, and whined.

Cooper laughed. "Come on," he said. "Let's give Brutus a steak for all his help, and take him home. And then we need to drop in on Mother and Ken—" He kissed her slowly and thoroughly. "And break the news that they're soon going to have to share the Lovers' Box."

PARENTS WANTED

Families in the making!

In the orphanage of a small Australian town called Bay Beach are little children desperately in need of love, and dreaming of their very own family....

The answer to their dreams can also be found in Bay Beach! Couples who are destined for each other—even if they don't know it yet. Brought together by love for these tiny children, can they find true love themselves— and finally become a real family?

Titles in this series by fan-favorite **MARION LENNOX** are

A Child in Need—(April HR #3650)
Their Baby Bargain—(July HR #3662)

Look out for further Parents Wanted stories in Harlequin Romance®, coming soon!

Available wherever Harlequin Books are sold.

If you enjoyed what you just read,
then we've got an offer you can't resist!

Take 2 bestselling love stories FREE!

Plus get a FREE surprise gift!

Clip this page and mail it to Harlequin Reader Service®

IN U.S.A.	IN CANADA
3010 Walden Ave.	P.O. Box 609
P.O. Box 1867	Fort Erie, Ontario
Buffalo, N.Y. 14240-1867	L2A 5X3

YES! Please send me 2 free Harlequin Romance® novels and my free surprise gift. Then send me 6 brand-new novels every month, which I will receive months before they're available in stores. In the U.S.A., bill me at the bargain price of $2.90 plus 25¢ delivery per book and applicable sales tax, if any*. In Canada, bill me at the bargain price of $3.34 plus 25¢ delivery per book and applicable taxes**. That's the complete price and a savings of 10% off the cover prices—what a great deal! I understand that accepting the 2 free books and gift places me under no obligation ever to buy any books. I can always return a shipment and cancel at any time. Even if I never buy another book from Harlequin, the 2 free books and gift are mine to keep forever. So why not take us up on our invitation. You'll be glad you did!

186 HEN C4GY
386 HEN C4GZ

Name	(PLEASE PRINT)	
Address	Apt.#	
City	State/Prov.	Zip/Postal Code

* Terms and prices subject to change without notice. Sales tax applicable in N.Y.
** Canadian residents will be charged applicable provincial taxes and GST.
All orders subject to approval. Offer limited to one per household.
® are registered trademarks of Harlequin Enterprises Limited.

HROM00_R2   ©1998 Harlequin Enterprises Limited

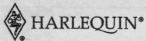

HARLEQUIN *Super*ROMANCE®

To celebrate the
1000th Superromance book
We're presenting you with 3 books
from 3 of your favorite authors in

All Summer Long

Home, Hearth and Haley
by **Muriel Jensen**

Meet the men and women of Muriel's
upcoming **Men of Maple Hill** trilogy

Daddy's Girl
by **Judith Arnold**

Another **Daddy School** story!

Temperature Rising
by **Bobby Hutchinson**

Life and love at St. Joe's Hospital are as feverish
as ever in this **Emergency!** story

On sale July 2001
Available wherever Harlequin books are sold.

HARLEQUIN®
Makes any time special ®

*Harlequin truly does
make any time special....
This year we are celebrating
weddings in style!*

A
Walk
Down
the Aisle
WEDDING CELEBRATION

To help us celebrate, we want you to tell us how wearing the Harlequin wedding gown will make your wedding day special. As the grand prize, Harlequin will offer one lucky bride the chance to **"Walk Down the Aisle"** in the Harlequin wedding gown!

There's more...

For her honeymoon, she and her groom will spend five nights at the **Hyatt Regency Maui.** As part of this five-night honeymoon at the hotel renowned for its romantic attractions, the couple will enjoy a candlelit dinner for two in Swan Court, a sunset sail on the hotel's catamaran, and duet spa treatments.

A HYATT RESORT AND SPA

Maui • Molokai • Lanai

To enter, please write, in, 250 words or less, how wearing the Harlequin wedding gown will make your wedding day special. The entry will be judged based on its emotionally compelling nature, its originality and creativity, and its sincerity. This contest is open to Canadian and U.S. residents only and to those who are 18 years of age and older. There is no purchase necessary to enter. Void where prohibited. See further contest rules attached. Please send your entry to:

Walk Down the Aisle Contest

In Canada	In U.S.A.
P.O. Box 637	P.O. Box 9076
Fort Erie, Ontario	3010 Walden Ave.
L2A 5X3	Buffalo, NY 14269-9076

You can also enter by visiting www.eHarlequin.com
Win the Harlequin wedding gown and the vacation of a lifetime!
The deadline for entries is October 1, 2001.

HARLEQUIN®
Makes any time special ®

PHWDACONT1

HARLEQUIN WALK DOWN THE AISLE TO MAUI CONTEST 1197
OFFICIAL RULES
NO PURCHASE NECESSARY TO ENTER

1. To enter, follow directions published in the offer to which you are responding. Contest begins April 2, 2001, and ends on October 1, 2001. Method of entry may vary. Mailed entries must be postmarked by October 1, 2001, and received by October 8, 2001.

2. Contest may be, at times, presented via the Internet, but will be restricted solely to residents of certain geographic areas that are disclosed on the Web site. To enter via the Internet, if permissible, access the Harlequin Web site (www.eHarlequin.com) and follow the directions displayed online. Online entries must be received by 11:59 p.m. E.S.T. on October 1, 2001.

   In lieu of submitting an entry online, enter by mail by hand-printing (or typing) on an 8½" x 11" plain piece of paper, your name, address (including zip code), Contest number/name and in 250 words or fewer, why winning a Harlequin wedding dress would make your wedding day special. Mail via first-class mail to: Harlequin Walk Down the Aisle Contest 1197, (in the U.S.) P.O. Box 9076, 3010 Walden Avenue, Buffalo, NY 14269-9076, (in Canada) P.O. Box 637, Fort Erie, Ontario L2A 5X3, Canada.

   Limit one entry per person, household address and e-mail address. Online and/or mailed entries received from persons residing in geographic areas in which Internet entry is not permissible will be disqualified.

3. Contests will be judged by a panel of members of the Harlequin editorial, marketing and public relations staff based on the following criteria:

   - Originality and Creativity—50%
   - Emotionally Compelling—25%
   - Sincerity—25%

   In the event of a tie, duplicate prizes will be awarded. Decisions of the judges are final.

4. All entries become the property of Torstar Corp. and will not be returned. No responsibility is assumed for lost, late, illegible, incomplete, inaccurate, nondelivered or misdirected mail or misdirected e-mail, for technical, hardware or software failures of any kind, lost or unavailable network connections, or failed, incomplete, garbled or delayed computer transmission or any human error which may occur in the receipt or processing of the entries in this Contest.

5. Contest open only to residents of the U.S. (except Puerto Rico) and Canada, who are 18 years of age or older, and is void wherever prohibited by law; all applicable laws and regulations apply. Any litigation within the Province of Quebec respecting the conduct or organization of a publicity contest may be submitted to the Régie des alcools, des courses et des jeux for a ruling. Any litigation respecting the awarding of a prize may be submitted to the Régie des alcools, des courses et des jeux only for the purpose of helping the parties reach a settlement. Employees and immediate family members of Torstar Corp. and D. L. Blair, Inc., their affiliates, subsidiaries and all other agencies, entities and persons connected with the use, marketing or conduct of this Contest are not eligible to enter. Taxes on prizes are the sole responsibility of winners. Acceptance of any prize offered constitutes permission to use winner's name, photograph or other likeness for the purposes of advertising, trade and promotion on behalf of Torstar Corp., its affiliates and subsidiaries without further compensation to the winner, unless prohibited by law.

6. Winners will be determined no later than November 15, 2001, and will be notified by mail. Winners will be required to sign and return an Affidavit of Eligibility form within 15 days after winner notification. Noncompliance within that time period may result in disqualification and an alternative winner may be selected. Winners of trip must execute a Release of Liability prior to ticketing and must possess required travel documents (e.g. passport, photo ID) where applicable. Trip must be completed by November 2002. No substitution of prize permitted by winner. Torstar Corp. and D. L. Blair, Inc., their parents, affiliates, and subsidiaries are not responsible for errors in printing or electronic presentation of Contest, entries and/or game pieces. In the event of printing or other errors which may result in unintended prize values or duplication of prizes, all affected game pieces or entries shall be null and void. If for any reason the Internet portion of the Contest is not capable of running as planned, including infection by computer virus, bugs, tampering, unauthorized intervention, fraud, technical failures, or any other causes beyond the control of Torstar Corp. which corrupt or affect the administration, secrecy, fairness, integrity or proper conduct of the Contest, Torstar Corp. reserves the right, at its sole discretion, to disqualify any individual who tampers with the entry process and to cancel, terminate, modify or suspend the Contest or the Internet portion thereof. In the event of a dispute regarding an online entry, the entry will be deemed submitted by the authorized holder of the e-mail account submitted at the time of entry. Authorized account holder is defined as the natural person who is assigned to an e-mail address by an Internet access provider, online service provider or other organization that is responsible for arranging e-mail address for the domain associated with the submitted e-mail address. **Purchase or acceptance of a product offer does not improve your chances of winning.**

7. Prizes: (1) Grand Prize—A Harlequin wedding dress (approximate retail value: $3,500) and a 5-night/6-day honeymoon trip to Maui, HI, including round-trip air transportation provided by Maui Visitors Bureau from Los Angeles International Airport (winner is responsible for transportation to and from Los Angeles International Airport) and a Harlequin Romance Package, including hotel accomodations (double occupancy) at the Hyatt Regency Maui Resort and Spa, dinner for (2) two at Swan Court, a sunset sail on Kiele V and a spa treatment for the winner (approximate retail value: $4,000); (5) Five runner-up prizes of a $1000 gift certificate to selected retail outlets to be determined by Sponsor (retail value $1000 ea.). Prizes consist of only those items listed as part of the prize. Limit one prize per person. All prizes are valued in U.S. currency.

8. For a list of winners (available after December 17, 2001) send a self-addressed, stamped envelope to: Harlequin Walk Down the Aisle Contest 1197 Winners, P.O. Box 4200 Blair, NE 68009-4200 or you may access the www.eHarlequin.com Web site through January 15, 2002.

Contest sponsored by Torstar Corp., P.O. Box 9042, Buffalo, NY 14269-9042, U.S.A.

PHWDACONT2